J. T. EDSON

WACO'S DEBT

CORGI BOOKS
TRANSWORLD PUBLISHERS LTD
A National General Company

WACO'S DEBT

A CORGI BOOK 552 07899 9

Originally published in Great Britain
by Brown Watson Ltd.

PRINTING HISTORY
Corgi Edition published 1968
Corgi Edition reprinted 1969
Corgi Edition reprinted 1972

This book is set in
Baskerville 9 on 11 pt.

Corgi Books are published by Transworld Publishers, Ltd.,
Cavendish House, 57–59 Uxbridge Road, Ealing,
London, W.5.

Made and printed in Great Britain by
Richard Clay (The Chaucer Press), Ltd., Bungay, Suffolk

CHAPTER ONE

OLE DEVIL GIVES THE WORD

IT was a man's room. The furniture was good and comfortable but without any of the softer frills a woman would give to it. Over the big open-fronted fireplace hung the battleflag of the Confederated States of America, the Stars and Bars. Flanking the bullet-scarred flag hung two cavalry pennants, each also marked by bullets. Beneath them, obviously in a place of honour, was a shining, polished oak box, the lid open, the red felt caressing and holding two magnificently chased, pearl-butted and gold inlaid Colt Cavalry Peacemakers. On the lid of the box was a brass plate with the inscription:

COCHISE COUNTY FAIR PISTOL SHOOT
WINNER
CAPTAIN DUSTY FOG

Fanning out from the flags, hung on pegs, were revolvers and pistols. The line of Colt revolvers, from the first Paterson model, up through the Walker, the Dragoons, the Navies, the Wells Fargo, the conversion of the 1860 Army cap and ball by Richardson or by Thuer, the Peacemaker and the Lightning. Beyond them were other handguns, single-shot Remington cartridge guns, deadly pistols of a bygone age. There, mixed among the others, looking like a sawed-off Winchester rifle with a pistol butt, was a Volcanic; next to it a European-made ten-shot, pinfire revolver, smuggled through the Yankee blockade to aid the arms-starved Confederacy.

The man who sat in the wheelchair fitted well into this martial setting. He was tall, spare and hard looking. Not even the years he'd spent in the wheelchair had bowed his shoulders or relaxed the ramrod straight back in the coat of a Confederate Army General. His lean, tanned, fighting man's face, the eyes black and piercing, the hooked nose and the tight, firm mouth with the tiniest hint of a grin at the corners, showed nothing of self-pity. He sat his chair as he'd always sat his horse, straight, and with the air of a man long used to command. He was Ole Devil Hardin, owner of the biggest ranch in this section of Texas, if not the biggest in the whole of the Lone Star State.

Right now he was relaxing, frosty eyes looking down unseeing at the book on his lap, mate to the many on the shelves at the far end of the room. He was, perhaps, thinking of the days when he commanded the Texas Light Cavalry in the War Between The States. Whatever the reason for his reverie, he paid no attention when the door opened behind him.

'Is there any word from Dusty yet, sir?'

The voice, an easy and even Texas drawl, came from behind him, and brought him swinging the chair around to look at the speaker. The black eyes showed nothing of his thoughts, but his lips broke in a rare smile at the words. It was so like young Waco to ask this. He'd asked it nearly every day since the Rio Hondo gun wizard, Dusty Fog, left with a herd for Texas John Slaughter over to Cochise County, Arizona. Waco gave to Dusty Fog the loyalty, devotion and hero-worship which would have gone to his father, had not Waco Indians left him an orphan almost from birth.

'I heard from him when the mail came in this morning, boy. The Kid's not fit enough to ride just yet, about another week and they'll be on their way back home.'

Waco grinned at this. He was still hoping for a chance to saddle his big paint stallion and head for Escopeta County, New Mexico, and help Dusty Fog and Mark Counter find the men who shot down the Ysabel Kid. Now there was going to be no excuse for it and he would have to carry on his work with the floating outfit here at the O.D. Connected.

He was a tall, young man, over six foot, with wide shoulders and a lean, trim waist. His face was tanned by the elements, handsome and young looking, his blond hair curly and taken straight back. In dress he could be mistaken for nothing but

6

what he was; a Texas cowhand and a good one at that. He'd hung his low-crowned, wide-brimmed J. B. Stetson on the peg behind the door and was now hanging up the buscadero gunbelt on the hook, the matched, staghorn-butted Colt Artillery Peacemakers in the holsters. Around his throat was a tight-rolled, long, blue silk bandana, the ends falling down over his dark blue shirt and calfskin vest. His brown levis hung outside his high-heeled, fancy-stitched and costly boots. The boots themselves had Kelly spurs at the heels and were real, genuine Justins.

After his query into Dusty Fog's welfare, Waco crossed the room and sat at a side table, taking up the deck of cards which lay on the table ready for use. Two more men followed him into the room and were hanging their hats on the hooks.

The first was as tall as Waco, just as well built, though not so trimmed down towards the hips. His hair was a violent red, curly, rumpled and untidy as if it rarely felt the mercies of comb and brush. His face was freckled, tanned and handsome, a happy untroubled face. His clothes showed him to be as much a Texas cowhand as Waco and, unless the sign read wrong, one of the top water. The bandana around his throat was of silk and brilliantly coloured. He stripped the heavy gunbelt with the twin, walnut-handled Colt Cavalry Peacemakers butt forward in the holsters, and put it under his hat.

The last of the trio was also tall, though not as tall as Waco or Red Blaze. He was slimmer, his face studious, pallid with a tan-resisting pallor, mild almost. Yet for all of that he wore the dress of a tophand cowboy and the gunbelt around his waist, with the ivory-butted Colt Civilian Peacemaker at his right side spelled only one thing. Here was a fast man with a gun. The only difference between this man, Doc Leroy and the other two was that he invariably wore a brown coat, the right side stitched back to leave him clear and fast access to his gun.

These three young men, Waco, Red Blaze and Doc Leroy were members of the elite of the O.D. Connected Ole Devil's floating outfit. They, along with Dusty Fog, Mark Counter and the Ysabel Kid, were the floating outfit, picked men, skilled

7

with cattle and all branches of the cattle industry, but also skilled in the use of their guns. They alone of the ranch crew had access to this room here, Ole Devil's library. Here Waco spent much of his spare time, improving his education from the books in the library, cleaning or just examining the guns, or playing poker with Doc Leroy, practising the skills of a crooked gambler.

Right now, poker was in the offing and Waco gave the cards a fast riffle stack then said, 'You playing, Red?'

'Not me, boy. I like to play fair when I play.'

Waco chuckled and gave the cards a fast riffle again, passing them to Doc to cut. Doc was no mean hand with the paste-boards himself and their games were not so much poker playing as a battle of wits as each tried to outcheat the other.

Red Blaze joined his uncle, answering questions about the work they'd done on the range that day. Then he took up a newspaper which lay on the table and opened it out. The front page was typical of the day, nothing out of the ordinary on it. He looked down the columns where the news was recorded and an editorial damned Sam Bass's efforts at train robbery. Then another item caught his eye.

'You hail from the Ranse country, don't you, Waco?'

'That where I started out from,' Waco agreed as he flipped a desired card from the centre of the deck for the first time without Doc detecting him.

'There's a rancher been murdered up there. Him and his two sons. Name of Sunshine Sam Catlan——'

The cards fell from Waco's hands. He thrust back his chair and came to his feet. His usually expressionless face was hard and set and his voice brittle and cold. 'What did you say, Red?'

Crossing the room Waco took the paper and looked down the columns of print until he saw what Red was talking about. His hands were not as steady as they usually were as he read the item:

PROMINENT RANCHER MURDERED

Today in Hood City, County Seat of Ranse River County, a

verdict of murder by person or persons unknown was brought by coroner's jury investigating the murder of rancher Sunshine Sam Catlan and his two sons, Race and Matthew. Sunshine Sam was noted for ...

Waco read on through the article, his face losing colour and turning pale under the tan. He crushed the paper in his powerful hands without even knowing what he was doing as he stood still, swaying slightly. Red caught the youngster's arm, steadying him and easing him into a chair.

'What is it, boy?' Ole Devil's voice cut in gently.

Waco's head was bowed for a moment then he got a grip of himself and looked up, face drawn. 'Sunshine Sam and his family raised me after the Indians got my folks. They'd nine kids of their own, but they still took me in. Lost all the kids 'cepting Race, Matt and Mary Anne. They lost all the others, Indians, illness, accidents. Yet they always treated me just like I was their own. Mary Anne, she was eighteen months older'n me and she looked after me. Used to call me her baby brother. Sam had him some bad luck, lost the kids, then just after I pulled out on my own he made him a killing in a poker game, started to build up the S.S.C. Made it real big, made it by hard work. I always aimed to go back up there and see them again but I never did.'

Red smoothed out the paper, cursing himself for being all kinds of a fool. It must have hit Waco hard, being told that the man who raised him was murdered. He read the article and said, 'Says here that Mary Anne's in school back in St. Louis and they've sent for her to come back. This paper's a week old and the killing took place three days afore that. She'll be nearly on home, not more than a couple of days off it at most.'

'You'd best go along, boy. She's going to need some help.'

Waco hardly understood Ole Devil's quiet spoken words. He was shocked more than ever before in his life. Since he was thirteen he'd ridden with death as a constant companion but never before did it strike so close to him. Sunshine Sam was the only kin he'd ever known. He'd taken him in and made

9

him one of the family; he and his wife couldn't have treated Waco better had he been one of their own. Now out of all his family only Mary Anne was left. Sunshine Sam's wife went the year before, according to the paper. Now Mary Anne his little Rusty gal, was alone in the world, going back to the S.S.C. She was going to need a lot of help now her father was dead, murdered by person or persons unknown. Then slowly the meaning of what Ole Devil said came through his jumbled thoughts. Ole Devil was giving him permission to go off; at this time when they were all needed here at the ranch he was allowing a tophand to go off on a mission which might take any length of time. He started to stammer out his thanks, the words coming awkwardly from his usually glib tongue.

Ole Devil waved the thanks aside and snapped, 'Red, tell Kiowa he'll take over as *segundo* and handle your work for a piece. Doc, check over your gear and see if there's anything you need. If there's anything at all you want go collect it from town. You'll be riding from here at sunup tomorrow.'

Waco could hardly believe his ears. It was now, more than ever before, that he realised why the men of the O.D. Connected would gladly have died for this hard-faced man who ruled them with a rod of iron. Not only was Ole Devil allowing him to go to Ranse River County, but he was also sending along two men who would be of the greatest use in case the murderers of Sunshine Sam Catlan wanted to get the rest of the Catlan family.

'I—er, I——' Waco began again, trying to show his gratitude to Ole Devil. Red and Doc were his friends and they were the ones he would want along with him in this, with Dusty Fog, Mark Counter and the Ysabel Kid not being here.

'You've got some riding to do, Doc,' Ole Devil Hardin cut in before Waco could finish. 'Go make your check. Red, head down right now and see Kiowa.' The two turned and left the room and Ole Devil gave his full attention to Waco who was still seated in the chair and staring, without really seeing, at the paper before him. 'All right now, boy. You stay here and tell me all about Sunshine Sam Catlan.'

CHAPTER TWO

MARY ANNE COMES HOME...

'I'LL give five to one she sells, boys!'

Doctor Henry J. Smethers, sole medico for Ranse River County, glared at the speaker, his usually mild, sun-reddened face showing some anger. The woman who was shouting this speech stopped, studied the doctor for a moment, then came forward with her hand held out in a warm and friendly greeting.

'Why Doc,' she said winningly, 'We don't often see you in here.'

Della Christine was a beautiful woman and knew it. It showed in the arrogant way her blonde hair was piled up on top of her head, in the beautiful, almost flawless contours of the face with the pouting, sulky lips. It showed in the skin-tight, figure-showing red dress, a dress which was slit to the hip on one side showing her black stockinged shapely legs to anyone who wished to look at them. She wanted them to look, for Della Christine lived only for the admiring glances of men.

Doc Smethers was one man who did not admire her. He was a small, cheery, bald man, fat and passing middle-age. His town clothes were rumpled, his shirt open at the neck and tieless. His admiration for Della was not so large as other men's for he was not fooled by her. She was something he'd seen from New Orleans to San Francisco and back the long way, a woman preying on the woman-hungry men. It was the way she made her living, and Della Christine was good at it.

The saloon here, Della's Tavern, was not what one would expect in a small Texas cattle town. There hardly appeared to be sufficient trade for so garish a place. Smethers thought that

11

when the place was built a few months before. It was bigger than most every other place in town, a two storey construction which dwarfed the surrounding buildings on Whittle Town's Front Street. The saloon inside kept up with the pretentious appearance of the outside, the gaming tables as good or better than could be found even in Hood City, the county seat. The bar was long and of shining mahogany; behind it an array of bottles and a long mirror which showed the whole of the room. It was surprising that such a place should be here in this small town, for there did not appear to be any use or need for it.

'I see you're betting that Mary Anne Catlan sells the S.S.C.' Doc ignored the hand, his voice mild compared with Della's strident tones.

'Sure, Doc,' Della threw back her head and laughed. 'What would a milk-faced dude like her want with a ranch?'

Smethers held down a smile. Mary Anne Catlan was far from a milk-faced dude. She'd been as wild and reckless a tomboy as could be found in the West. The Catlan family were proud of her prowess on the back of a horse or in a hair-yanking battle with some other girl. She'd been sent to the Eastern school in the hope it would teach her the social graces which Sunshine Sam thought she needed. Today she was due back; would be coming in on the stage which would soon arrive.

Doc studied Della for a moment, then said, 'I'll lay fifty dollars on that, with you.'

'It's a real foolish chance, Doc,' Della answered.

'I doubt it. Besides I make enough when Brarsand's guns shoot each other up.'

Della frowned. She did not like Smethers' attitude. She was used to respect from men and the old doctor never showed her any. She did not care for anyone talking in such a manner about her boss, Carl Brarsand. Her fingers drummed on the bar as she frowned at Doc, then she said something which under normal circumstances she would not have thought of saying:

'All right then, Doc. If you're so sure I'll make another bet

12

with you. If she stays I'll drag her out of town by the hair.'

Smethers was turning to leave the bar but he came around with a grin on his face. 'I'll have another fifty on that. Let me know when you aim to try and I'll get ready to do some work.'

'On her when I've finished with her?'

'On you. If you try a thing like that with Mary Anne Catlan she'll whip you so fast you'll think the hawgs have jumped you.' Saying this, Smethers raised his hat to the woman and walked from the saloon with a swagger in his stride.

Della scowled after him. Somehow every time she tried to out-talk the old man she was left standing and wondering what went wrong. Then she felt a hand grip her arm and turned. Her boss, Carl Brarsand, stood by her side, annoyance plain on his face. He was a big man, tall, heavy and handsome. His clothes were cut to the latest Eastern style, but under his arm there was a bulge which spelled shoulder holster to eyes which could see the signs.

'What's going on here, Della?' he asked.

'Just a little bit of fun for the boys,' Della answered, her voice whining and frightened. 'Betting she sells out. You know we need some money towards running this place.'

His fingers bit hard into the firm flesh of her arm. 'You stupid cow. We don't need money that bad. Look, we've built this place so we're ready when the town booms open. We don't want folks talking about us.'

'All right,' Della sounded scared and she had need to be for Brarsand was a vile-tempered man when crossed. 'Did you see Doc Pilsener in Chicago?'

'Yeah. He did it for us. I sent the letter off as soon as it was done. It should be here either today or tomorrow, then I'll go and see O'Rea, and make him an offer.'

'How about Doc, will he talk?' Della watched the big man's face.

'No, he won't talk.' Brarsand instinctively patted the bulge under his left shoulder.

Smethers stamped along the street towards the smaller and not so pretentious bar of the Hood City Saloon. He pushed open the batwing doors and entered the small, dark and cool

13

bar-room. Only two men were in here at the moment. One was Jabe Spencer, the owner, a short, and cheerful man. The other was tall and lean, wore range clothes and belted a low-tied Leech and Rigdon percussion-fired revolver which had seen some use. He was Lafe Sanger, once town marshal, now reduced by the arrival of a younger man, to jailer.

'A glass of your Old Scalp Raiser, Jabe!' Doc bellowed as he came across the room. 'I've just made us some money.'

'Man can always use it, Doc,' Spencer answered.

'What's up, Doc?' Sanger went on.

'I was just in Brarsand's place to collect a bill, him having been away for a few days. Della's betting Mary Anne Catlan sells out. Then she bet that she'll run Mary Anne out of town personal if she don't sell and go.'

Two startled faces looked at Doc, faces in which delight started to show. It was Sanger who spoke first, 'I surely hopes you lay some on for us two.'

'Thirty dollars each.'

Thirty dollars was a lot of money to the two men, but they did not appear to be worried by it. They knew Mary Anne Catlan and were willing to take more than just that much on her in a matter of this kind.

'Them bunch there allows they're some slick,' Spencer whooped. 'They don't know ole Mary Anne.'

'Remember the bay Jack Wilmont bought?' Sanger went on. 'His Molly and Mary Anne tried to ride it. I reckon it piled them both five times, but every time one of them was throwed the other got on it. They licked that hoss between them.'

'The only thing they couldn't lick was each other and they sure tried often enough,' Smethers remarked. 'Now Molly's in Chicago and letting ole Whit Dwyer run the ranch for her. I wish she'd come back now, what with Mary Anne coming home and Sunshine Sam getting killed out there on the Ranse.'

'I wonder who killed Sam and his boys,' Sangster spoke gently. 'It wasn't one of them nester families on the other side of the river. You handled the inquest, didn't you, Doc?'

'Sure.' Doc appeared to be wanting to change the subject.

'The gal needs help. There ain't nobody she could turn to now except maybe you two and Colonel O'Dea. But the ranch crew needs them a leader and she can't give them that.'

Pulling his watch out Sanger glanced at it and grunted. 'Stage's just about due in, let's go and see it.'

'Sure, let's show ole Mary Anne she ain't alone.'

The three men finished their drinks and walked out of the saloon, back along the street to where, facing Della's Tavern, the Wells Fargo stageline office stood. A crowd was gathering to greet the westbound stage, the event of the day. Sanger noticed that the saloon crowd were on the sidewalk in front of Della's Tavern, Della with them. So was Brarsand, the old-timer noted and wondered where the handsome man had been for the last few days. He'd left soon after the death of Catlan, Sanger recalled and only returned this day or early yesterday. He lounged by the door of the saloon, around him seven or eight hard-looking, gunhung men who worked on the payroll of his saloon.

Sanger's thoughts on the owner of Della's Tavern were distracted by the arrival of the stagecoach. It came hurtling along the street and halted in front of the office. The door opened, a flashily-dressed whisky drummer jumped out, turned and held out his hand to the young woman who came to the door. The watching men were amazed at the charge in her for they recognised Mary Anne Catlan.

She'd gone away a tanned, happy-go-lucky tomboy and come back a lady. Mary Anne Catlan stood on the sidewalk, her cheeks were no longer tanned by the elements, but soft and delicate. She was a tall mature girl, as tall as Della Christine and with a figure, which, while not being so openly displayed, was just as rich and full. She wore a small, eastern-style hat on her elegantly cared for rusty red hair, her face was innocent of makeup and her black dress plain yet stylish. In her right had she held a vanity bag which she toyed with as she looked around at the familiar sights of her home. There was a twinkle in her eye as she saw the three men converging on her.

'Good to see you, Mary Anne gal,' Sanger said, moving

15

forward and holding out his big hand to her. The coach was moving now, making its way around the side of the building to off-load mail and luggage.

Mary Anne sighed. 'The ride completely fatigued me. I cannot imagine how anyone could stand to travel further in such a bumpy vehicle. It really was too much for me.'

The three men exchanged looks. This from a girl who'd ridden many miles on the back of a half-wild cowhorse. Sanger gulped, then went on. 'We've got that old dun hoss of your'n down at the saloon. Had him brought in from the spread for you, thought you'd want to ride him back.'

'Goodness me!' Marry Anne sounded horrified. 'Ride a dangerous creature like that. I will hire a buckboard and a gentle team, then get a driver to take me home.'

Brarsand and Della could hear every word being said and the blonde sniggered. 'I could go over there right now and win both them bets.'

'You stand here and keep your mouth shut,' Brarsand snapped back. 'We'll handle it the way I fixed it.' With this he nodded to a man who lounged against the wall at the end of the saloon.

The man lurched forward from the porch, moving like he'd taken on too much bravemaker and was set to have him some fun. He crossed the street by the waterbutt which stood, full and ready for use on the dirt street, just in front of the Wells Fargo office. Swinging up on to the porch he halted and looked owlishly at Mary Anne, then grinned. 'A redhead. I likes redheads. Going to have me a kiss.'

Sanger was about to lunge forward and intervene as the man came at Mary Anne with his arms held out to enfold and hug her. Suddenly the sedate mildness left Mary Anne and her eyes flashed with the fire of sudden anger. She swung her arm, bringing the bag around to smash into the side of the man's head. For a blow with a vanity bag it looked to pack unseemly power. The man staggered backwards and from the pain and the way his head spun he knew there was more than just ladylike trifles in that bag. His suspicions were proved when Mary Anne's other hand shot into the bag and emerged with

16

an item that should not have been in the possession of a milk-faced dude girl. He snarled out a curse, but his lunge forward came to an abrupt halt as Mary Anne gave an order.

'Stop right where you are.' Her voice was changed from the bored elegant tones to a hard, clipped-down Texas drawl that brooked no argument.

The man stayed where he was. He always did as requested. The Merwin and Hulbert gun in Mary Anne's grip was pointed right at him, pointed and held by a hand which was used to doing such things, the .45 bore of the short barrel was lined right at his stomach. Short barrelled or not it would make a hell of a mess of him if the girl was anything like a shot and she gave the impression she was.

'Sorry lady,' the man's voice was sober now, sober and worried. 'I was only funning——'

'Drift and *pronto*!'

The man gulped. From the way the girl talked now she knew the range country well. He turned on his heel and shambled away, followed by the laughter and jeers of the crowd. Mary Anne let him go, throwing back her head and roaring with unladylike laughter as she pushed the gun back into her bag again. She turned to Sanger who was shoving his old gun back into leather after drawing it ready to put a .36 ball where it would have done the most good.

It was the old Mary Anne Catlan who looked at them; 'Lordy me, your faces when I started talking to you,' she finally gasped out. 'I thought I'd play it that way and see how you acted.'

'You surely had us fooled, gal,' Spencer grinned back. 'I thought you'd gone all eastern dude.'

The smile faded for a moment. 'Where did you bury pappy and the boys, Lafe?'

'In that grove with the others,' Sanger answered. 'I——'

'That's all right. I'm over the worst of it now. Pappy wouldn't want me to start sniffing.'

Brarsand was crossing the street now with Della following on his heels, a disturbed look in her eyes. He came to a stop in front of Mary Anne, swept off his hat and said, 'Welcome home, Miss Catlan. May I congratulate you on the way you handled that drunken cowhand.' He shot a look at the three men. 'I would like to see you alone.'

'I've known Lafe, Jabe and Doc for more years than I can count. If they can't hear what you've got to say to me, I don't want to.' Mary Anne took an instant and completely inexplicable dislike to the man. It was the western girl's natural aversion to a fancy-dressed dude.

'I would much rather speak to you alone.'

'And I'd rather you didn't.' Mary Anne saw the saloon woman's face redden. The crowd was dispersing now, seeing there was nothing more dramtic likely to be happening. 'Tell it, mister. I want to be on the way to the S.S.C. in time to get there before dark.'

'All right then.' Brarsand held down his anger. 'I would like to make you an offer for the S.S.C.'

'It's not for sale.'

'I'll make you a good offer for it, Miss Catlan. You know, a young woman cannot run a large ranch like the S.S.C.'

Mary Anne shrugged. 'I can make a try. I didn't do too bad with that gunny of yours, did I?'

'My gunny?' Brarsand frowned, looking puzzled. 'I'm not sure what you mean. He was just a drunken cowhand.'

'He wasn't drunk and he wasn't a cowhand,' Mary Anne contradicted. 'I saw you wigwag to him just before he came across here.'

'You saw too damned much!' Della hissed. She was fast losing her temper, for she could see she was costing Brarsand money. The ranch girl was not going to give things up.

Mary Anne looked the blonde up and down with a cold and contemptuous gaze, then, as if dismissing her as of no consequence, turned to the man again. 'You must have thought I was green, pulling a play like that. What was he supposed to do, make me think the wild, wild West was too wild and woolly for me.'

'Listen you——!' Della hissed, seeing Smethers watching her with a grin on his face.

'Ask your mother to keep out of this,' Mary Anne remarked.

Della snarled out a curse, pushing by Brarsand and lunging forward at the girl, hands reaching for her hair. Mary Anne's eyes flickered with the light of battle. She moved and acted in a manner which caught Della by surprise. Mary Anne's hands shot out and pulled with a strength that was out of all proportion to her size. Della shot forward and hit the hitching rail hard. She went right over the rail and fell head first into the water-butt. Della's angry squeal sounded as she went over, then died away as her head went under the greenish and stagnant water.

Mary Anne stood back with hands on hips and roared with laughter as she watched Della's legs waving. The laughter was echoed by every man in the street and it was some seconds before three of Brarsand's men came to pull her out. They had to help the winded, half-drowned, soaking and dishevelled woman across the street. Mary Anne watched them and then gave her attention to Brarsand again.

'Still think I can't run the S.S.C.?'

'It could be awkward and lonely out there. I hear your crew aren't too happy about working for a woman.' Brarsand could see this girl was going to be more trouble than he first expected.

'I'll chance it.'

'Why bother. With the money I'll pay, you could go east and live the life a young lady should. There is no reason why you should tie yourself to a place like that ranch.'

'Mister,' Mary Anne's voice was grim. 'My pappy took the S.S.C. back in the old days. He fought Kiowas, Comanches and rustlers. He rode trail-drives, worked twelve or fifteen hours a day to build the S.S.C. up. He built it for the family and I'm not letting his work go for nothing.'

'I approve of your determination.' Brarsand made a change in his stand. 'If I can send a man to help run your spread, I will do so. If I can help you in any other way, just let me know.'

'Thanks. After I've looked the spread over I'll maybe take you up on it.'

Brarsand raised his hat again and was about to go when

Smethers coughed and remarked. 'I made a couple of bets with Della.'

The big man turned back. His face working angrily, but he knew better than quarrel with a gambling debt. 'All right, Doc. How much did you put on?'

'One hundred. At five to one.'

Brarsand scowled, but he took out his wallet and peeled off six one hundred dollar bills, passing them over. Then he turned and crossed the street, entering the saloon. Mary Anne watched him go then turned back to her three friends. 'What was all that about, and who was he?'

'Name's Brarsand, owns the saloon there. Bought out the old Shannon Ranch in the back country early on, but he sold it again. What you going to do, gal?' Sanger asked.

'Head down to see Colonel O'Dea, then go to the ranch,' Mary Anne replied. 'Where's that old dun of mine?'

'Down at the O'Dea place. Took him there when we heard you'd be coming in today,' Sanger explained.

On the walk to the O'Dea house at the back of town Mary Anne tried to learn as much as she could about the death of her father. There was not much to tell. Sunshine Sam had been fishing on the bank of the Ranse River, after a big old bass. His sons, as usual, went along with him, and there they were, found shot in the back, all three of them.

The county sheriff made a thorough investigation of the matter but could find nothing to help him in the search. Sunshine Sam was a man liked by all who knew him.

The ranch crew were still working the spread, but they were uncertain as to their future and might not stay on now. Mary Anne knew full well the difficulties which were coming to her. She also knew a strong hand was needed to control them. She thought of the many friends her father made. One of them was a curly-haired, smiling young man called Sam Bass. He might come and help her, but he was being hunted for some train robberies.

It was then she remembered Waco. It was all of five years since he'd left home to see something of the world. She'd heard little enough of him in the time which followed, although

Sunshine Sam passed the word for his adoped son to come home when he'd got the ranch going again. If Waco heard he'd never shown up, although word had it he was riding for Clay Allison's C.A. outfit. The thought did not make her happy, for she knew something about the hardcase crew who rode for Allison. They were not the best sort of company a boy would get into. His men were noted for ability with cattle but more so for ability with a gun. One thing she did know, if Waco heard of her father's death, he would return and give her all the help he could. She only hoped her little brother would return to help her now. The three old men here were her loyal friends and there were other people in town who would stand by her. They were not cowhands, however, or if they were once, were now too old and stove-up to be of use to her. With the ranch crew she would need a young man to lead them. She wondered how she could get in touch with Waco.

CHAPTER THREE

A VOICE FROM THE PAST

MARY ANNE CATLAN rode towards the old ranch house with misgiving filling her. She'd found Colonel O'Dea, the lawyer in town, was along at the County Seat attending to business and his two daughters along with him. So, leaving her luggage at the O'Dea house, she'd changed into a tartan shirt and old jeans, then with her stetson on her head and high-heeled, fancy stitched boots on her feet, she got her dun horse and headed for home. She thrilled to the rapid beat of hooves and the feeling of the horse moving under her. Yet for all of that she was worried. There was a lump in her throat as she rode towards the long, low white house. From the right, its lighted front showing people were in, was the bunk-house. She could hear the sounds which told her the ranch crew were having fun in the usual rowdy cowhand manner.

Swinging from her horse she took it down to the corral and attended to it. Then with the dun looked after she returned to the house. A small, fat Chinese man looked out of the door, his eyes drawing even more narrow, then a grin split his face and her threw the door wide open. 'Miss Mary Anne.' There was pleasure and affection on his face which did not go with the meat cleaver he held in his hand. 'I thought you would be back today.'

'Why sure, Lee.' Mary Anne gripped the man's hand in her own, knowing she'd got one friend here who would stand by her. 'I came as soon as I heard.'

'Is bad business, Missy. Hands all scared, ready to give up if you not got good man to lead them.'

Mary Anne bit down the flood of tears which welled up

inside her as she entered the hall of the house. She stood for a moment just inside, then made her decision. She was going to show the men that a woman could handle the ranch here. Turning on her heel she stepped back out into the night, pausing to speak to Lee Chan, her cook.

'You got any chow yet, Lee?'

'Got plenty, knew you'd want it. You always did, Missy.'

The girl managed a smile. Good old Lee Chan. He would stand by her no matter what. She hoped the other men would be the same. Walking across the open space to the bunkhouse she tried to decide what course to adopt. All too well she knew cowhands, knew their ways and habits. This first meeting was vital, for it could make or ruin her chances with the men. She felt the weight of the Merwin & Hulbert revolver thrust in her waistband and wondered if she should take it to the house before going to see the men. She decided against it and walked to the door, listening for a moment to some of the choicer expressions being used inside, smiling, not blushing for she'd used the same expressions herself. She knew better than to open the door and walk in for there was no telling what embarrassing state of undress some of the men might be in.

'Come in, Lee,' a voice yelled in answer to her knock. 'We done got ole Larry tied down.'

Mary Anne knocked again and the door was thrown open. A tall, lithe-looking young man with an untidy thatch of hair glared out. 'What the hell, Lee——!' The words died off as he looked at the girl. 'Gee, I'm sorry, ma'am, I thought it was——' He paused again and turned to yell a warning to the others to keep their talk clean as there was a lady at the door. 'I tell you there's a sure enough lady at the door. So hush down will you. Sorry, ma'am, they don't mean nothing about it. The house is up there, if you want it, ma'am.'

'Yeah, I know,' Mary Anne liked the look of the young man. He was obviously a good cowhand and might make a loyal friend. 'Likely I knowed it afore you did. I'm Mary Anne Catlan. Your new boss.'

'You're Miss Catlan?' The cowhand's face showed surprise as he looked at her.

'So they tell me. My pappy sure spent some money raising the wrong gal if I'm not. Reckon I could talk to the rest of the boys?'

'Sure, ma'am, just hold it for a minute.' Stepping back the cowhand yelled a warning that Miss Catlan was here and coming to see them. Waiting until all the other of the eight hands were respectably attired, he opened the door. Entering the bunkhouse Mary Anne found the men all standing around. She studied them with a quick glance. They were all newcomers; not one could she remember from her last time at home. Yet they all looked like they knew the cattle business and they did not look the sort either to panic or be scared off. All they needed was a leader. Then they would stand by her, fight for her if they needed to do so. They were not a hardcase fighting crew, proddy and ready to hunt trouble though.

The bunkhouse showed the usual untidy state, clothes, boots and other gear scattered about in profusion. The table in the centre of the room was littered with old Police Gazettes and mail order catalogues. She shoved them into the centre and sat on the edge, legs swinging as she watched the men. They were giving her some attention and she guessed they liked what they saw.

'I'm your new boss. The name's Mary Anne. Who's been acting as *segundo*?'

'I have, ma'am.'

'Mary Anne,' the girl corrected the tall young man who'd answered the door and let her in.

'I am, I reckon, Mary Anne,' the cowhand answered. 'I'm Larry Beaumont.'

'Pleased to meet you, Larry. I'll get acquainted with the rest of you boys as soon as I've fed. Then tomorrow you can take me out to see the range, Larry.'

The young man opened his mouth to say something, then closed it again. He did not show the eagerness she'd expected. Yet he did not look as if he were a slacker, nor could she see any sign of the range work having been neglected since her father's death. She looked at the other men. Their faces showed the same thing. There was bad trouble coming on the range and they did not want to be led by a young woman fresh from the East.

The room was silent now and from outside came a sound which took Mary Anne's attention. The men heard it and exchanged glances, but none of them said a word. Mary Anne ran the tip of her tongue across her lips and wondered what four horses were doing coming to the ranch at this time of the night. She went to the window and tried to pierce the dark and see who was coming.

'Who is it, Larry?'

'I don't know, ma'am. We don't get many callers out here. There's been some night riding done, up at Wilmont's.'

'All right!' Mary Anne knew few men would travel at night unless they had a definite purpose. It could not be a good purpose either, not in the present state of affairs.

'Get your guns! We'll show 'em.' Mary Anne gave the order in a whoop, but the men did not make a move. She read the indecision on each face and knew what was holding them back. They needed a man to lead them. Anger flooded over her and Mary Anne Catlan could work up quite a temper when she was riled. Drawing the revolver from her waistband she hissed, 'If you're all scared, I'm not.'

With that she turned and flung herself to the bunkhouse door, tore it open and ran out into the night. Tears were filling her eyes as she ran from the bunkhouse. Through the mist of them she saw three riders, one leading a packhorse, approaching. She brought up the gun and fired a wild shot. The three riders brought their horses to a halt and left the saddles with a speed which showed they were not exactly unused to being shot at. One of them flung himself behind the water-trough while the other two disappeared into the shelter of the blacksmith's forge. Mary Anne suddenly realised she was exposed to their return fire, standing out in the open.

Inside the bunkhouse the men looked at each other. They heard the shot and Larry yelled, 'Come on, that gal's worth fighting for.' He dived forward, right over his single bunk, collecting the revolver from where it hung holstered on his gunbelt. Landing on his feet he went for the door with the gun in his hand. With a fresh look in their eyes the other men grabbed up their guns and ran for the door, following him.

Mary Anne stood in the dark. She was scared but did not give way to the fear. So far no bullet had been thrown her way but she knew the men were likely to start any time now. Then a voice from the past came floating to her, a voice she could barely recognise for it was both familiar and strange to her.

'Hey, Rusty gal. You never could shoot wuth a cuss so put up the gun or I'll get Molly Wilmont to come and take it from you.'

Mary Anne did not hear the bunkhouse door thrown open behind her. She could not believe what she was hearing either. Only the family ever called her Rusty and only one living person ever called her Rusty gal. The gun fell from her hand as she saw a tall man rise from behind the water-trough. For an instant she stood without moving, then ran forward to throw herself at the man.

It was at this moment the ranch crew ran from the bunkhouse ready to defend the girl. They saw Mary Anne running forward and throwing herself at one of the men, bringing him crashing to the ground. One of the cowhands was carrying a lantern and they dashed forward until the scene was lit by it. At the same moment a voice said, 'Hold it up, gents.'

The cowhands stopped in their tracks. They'd acted without thinking and now were in trouble. A tall, grinning young man came from the shadows of the forge, a Spencer carbine held hip high. Behind him stood a second tall young man holding a Colt. He gave his approval to the course of action his friend laid down.

'Sure, hold it up, she's doing all right.'

The cowhands could see what the slim man meant. Mary Anne was kneeling astride the man, shoving his expensive black stetson hat into his face and gasping out incoherent words. Then with a heave he threw her from him, came up and lifted her as if she were a baby. Turning, he walked towards the water-trough and held her over it.

'No—Waco—no!' Mary Anne screamed as she saw where she was. 'Don't you dare drop me in the——'

The rest ended in a wild shriek and splash as the tall man

let the girl fall into the water. The ranch crew prepared to hurl themselves at this man even in the face of the guns the others held. Before they could make a move they saw the girl was sitting up in the water and laughing. The tall, handsome young man who'd thrown her in stepped forward and helped her out again.

'Rusty gal, you haven't changed one lil bit,' he said, then glanced at the other two. 'All right, put them away. They ain't going to hurt you none.'

The red-headed cowhand laughed, lowered the hammer of his Spencer carbine and walked to where his horse stood. The big claybank stallion snorted and he avoided the nipping teeth, then slid the carbine into his saddleboot. The lantern light showed the brand the horse carried to the interested gaze of the watching cowhands. It was made of two letters, an O and a D, the straight edge of the D touching the side of the O. The cowhands read the brand correctly and eyed this redhead with more interest.

Mary Anne climbed from the water-trough and, laughing still, threw her arms around the man who had put her there, kissing him. She held on to him for a moment then he gently moved her back, smiling down at her and looking her over.

'Rusty gal,' he finally said. 'I'm sorry I couldn't get here afore this. These are my pards, Red Blaze and Doc Leroy.'

Talk rumbled up among the cowhands at the names for both were well-known. Red Blaze was known as a tophand with cattle, as a better than fair hossbuster and as wild a yahoo as ever helped tree a trailend town at the end of a drive. Doc Leroy's name was also known as a tophand. People also spoke of his medical skill; of how he treated the gunshot wounds, set the broken bones and pulled the teeth of the cowhands of the Wedge trail-drive crew, and how he removed a man's appendix with the aid of that most scientific of surgical instruments, a bowie knife, by the light of a lantern, out in the open air just north of the Salt Fork of the Brazos River.

Waco himself was not so well known to the cowhands, although in the time he'd been riding for Ole Devil's floating outfit he'd become known as a good man with cattle, or a gun.

Right now Waco was holding the girl's shoulders gently in his powerful hands, looking down at her face. 'I'm sorry I wasn't here when Pappy got his. I came as soon as I heard.'

'I know, boy.' Mary Anne winced as the fingers tightened on her shoulders. Then he released her and a mischievous grin flickered across her face. She moved back slightly, walking around him, looking him all over and halting so he stood between her and the water trough. 'I do declare you haven't growed a single inch. Just stand there and let me take a good look.'

Waco stood, his face impassive and showing nothing of his thoughts as the girl moved closer as if to make her comparison. Then suddenly she lunged forward with hands shooting out to push hard. At the last instant, Waco swayed aside and carried by her impetus she shot by him. She felt his hand catch the seat of her pants and gave a howl of rage as she was dumped head first into the water once more. She came out of it using some choice expressions which would have shocked Mrs. Dupre, principal of the school for young ladies she'd so recently attended.

'You tried that fool trick on me afore this,' Waco reminded her.

Climbing out Mary Anne laughed, standing hands on hips and throwing back her head. She could see the cowhands watching her and saw the difference in their faces now. Then she turned and held out a hand to Red and Doc, shaking with a firm grip. 'Thanks for coming and taking care of the boy. Thanks for coming out to help me, boys. Now I'm going up to the house to get changed. You got me all wet, Waco.'

'You always was, Rusty gal.' Waco gripped the girl's arm and they headed for the house.

Lee Chan stood at the door of the house staring at the girl as she came on to the porch, dripping water at every step. 'What happened, Missy Mary Anne?'

'I fell in the water-trough,' Mary Anne replied, grinning. 'Get a meal going at the chucksack, I'll be down when I'm changed. Make up three more beds here, Waco and his pards will be living at the house.'

'We can bunk down at the hawgpen with the crew if you

like,' Waco told the girl.

'I *don't* like. You'll stay here at the house, all three of you. Where are you going now?'

'Put up the hosses.'

'Pleased to see me again?'

'Sure, real pleased, gal.'

'Pleased enough to hay down my dun for me?' Mary Anne asked innocently.

'That pleased I'll never be,' Waco answered grinning. 'All right, I'll do it. But I won't like it.'

'I never knew you to like anything that spelled work.' Mary Anne headed for the bedroom before Waco had a chance to answer this last remark.

By the time Waco returned with his two friends and their duffle, the girl was changed into dry clothes and a pair of Kiowa moccasins.

She showed them to their rooms and then escorted them to the bunkhouse. The ranch crew were at the table when the girl came in with Waco, Red and Doc. Larry Beaumont pushed back his chair and went to the girl, drawing the chair at the head of the table back for her. She took her seat and looked at the men. Larry resumed his seat again and glanced at the three newcomers.

'You staying on here, Waco?'

'For a spell. If Rusty gal here'll have me.'

Mary Anne looked up, grinning. 'I've got enough trouble on my hands right now without that. Looks like I'm stuck with you though so I'll have to put up with it.'

'Why thank you most to death,' Waco replied. 'I can surely see you haven't changed a little mite.'

'You'll take over as *segundo* for a spell, Red,' Mary Anne ignored Waco. 'The boy's too young yet.'

The ranch crew, even Larry agreed with the girl's choice of foreman. Red knew the cattle business well, knew how to handle men. If it came to trouble he would be best able to deal with it. The atmosphere at the table was different now, laughter rose and talk welled up in the way it always did with a happy crew led by a strong man. There was a new light in every face, and Mary Anne felt better.

With the meal over, Waco and the rest sat around smoking and talking. The girl watched this young man she'd always regarded as her little brother, seeing how he'd matured. She liked what she saw. Here was no proddy rider for a hard outfit but a man wise in the ways of the west, a fighting man yet not one who would start a fight. There was a look about him now that she liked. She was proud to see her little brother in such good company.

Waco found himself by Larry and asked, 'Where did it happen?'

'You know that deep hole down on the Ranse?' Larry was not sure just how this tough young man figured, but guessed he knew Mary Anne more than just casually. 'It was there. Sunshine Sam and the boys went up to try and catch the big old bass there. You know the one I mean, Mary Anne?'

'Sure, ole Mossyhorn. He was there when you left home, boy. Biggest bass I ever saw.'

'Yeah, I remember him. He wasn't so big.'

'Bet you've never seen his beat,' Larry remarked, his eyes on Mary Anne all the time.

'Caught one bigger,' Waco replied, spreading his hands about a foot apart. 'He was that big.'

'That's not big for a bass,' Mary Anne snorted.

'That was the width between his eyes.'

There was a laugh at this from the men. They were looking at Waco with fresh respect now. They'd thought he was a fast gun and now they could see he was also a real friendly young gent. Red Blaze was also watching Mary Anne and guessed she was not wanting to talk about her father's death just at the moment. He decided it was time to change the subject and this sounded like a good time to do it.

'Ole Waco here got caught one time. We was in Langtry visiting Uncle Roy and we saw this hombre sitting fishing. Looking real unusual.'

'What's unusual about a man fishing?' Mary Anne asked without thinking and knew she'd let herself in a trap.

'He was fishing in a wooden bucket. So ole Waco here goes up and says, "Caught any?" and the feller says——'

'You're the fourth.' Mary Anne finished for him.

'Wrong, he said you're the fifth.'

Waco grinned amiably and started to spin a windy about catching a walleye the length of his arm. Others of the crew took it up, vying with each to spin the biggest fishing lie. The room sounded as it always used to in the old days when Sunshine Sam sat at the head of the board and kept the hands amused with his stories. Laughter rang out and the ranch crew looked more like cowhands.

Sitting back Waco watched the men. He approved of Mary Anne putting Red in command as *segundo*. That would leave him more free to make his investigation into the death of his adopted father and brothers. Right now though, there was no need for talk about it. There would be time to start in the morning.

Red suddenly stopped telling what amounted to the best biggest lie of the evening. He frowned and listened. The others also fell silent wondering what brought about this change in him. He came to his feet and went to the window. 'Douse the lights!' His voice showed the urgency of the matter. 'We got callers coming.'

The cowhands heard the sound then. Faintly, but growing louder at every minute, came the rumble of many hooves. Not one of the cowhands spoke but there was a difference in their silence now. They'd been worried and uncertain, now they were ready, willing and only waiting for orders. Mary Anne blew out the lamp on the table and Larry, hands slapping his gunless side, doused the other light.

The cookshack as they called it was actually a room in the back of the main house. The men were not armed, coming to a meal rarely called for it. Now they could hear the rumble of hooves they all wished they were carrying weapons. Yet there was no panic among them, just waiting for orders.

Red took charge of the situation, once more proving that while he was a hot-tempered, reckless young man who was likely to pitch into any fight he came across without much thought of consequences, he was cool and capable when the chips were down.

'Get to the bunkhouse, boys. Go the back way, run for it and get your guns. Then stay in, if you have to shoot do it from the windows.'

The cowhands made a rush for the door. Red, Waco and Doc went for the house door and ran along the passage towards the front door and the gunbelts hanging on the hooks. The hooves were very near now and Red doubted if they would be in time. He pulled one of his guns out, cocking it as he jerked the door open and lunged out. The porch was in the shadow, something he was grateful for. The moon was just gone the half and gave out enough light for him to see what he was doing.

There were nine or ten riders coming towards the ranch, riding fast, their identity covered by the hoods they wore over their heads. The leader of the group swung a blazing torch as he rode. Red and the other men on the porch watched this rider. He kept grabbing at the saddlehorn to keep his uncertain seat, riding awkwardly and without the unconscious grace even a bad drunk cowhand retained. There was something unusual about him, apart from his awkward way of riding. He did not appear to be wearing range clothes and was not wearing a gunbelt. There was a fancy, white-handled gun thrust into the waistband of his pants, but he did not make any attempt to draw it.

Red heard a gasp and twisted his head to see Mary Anne by his side watching the approaching party. He growled deep in his throat. 'Get back in there, gal. This's no place for you.'

Mary Anne did not reply or move, she was staring at the torch-waving man. He sent his horse forward at a better speed, swinging the torch around his head wildly. She licked her lips and was about to speak when she heard Red hiss, 'Just a little mite nearer, friend, and I'll bring you down like a coon off a log.'

The rider was coming just that little bit nearer, the other men crowding up behind him and encouraging him with wild yells. Then from the riders behind this first one sounded a shot. The man's back arched as lead hit him. He bowed his back in the sudden agony which welled up over him. Another rider was alongside, shooting out an arm to grab the torch and push the shot man from his saddle.

CHAPTER FOUR

A PROFESSIONAL'S GUN

THE shooting down of the man by a member of his own group made Red hold his fire for an instant. He could not see just what the attacking group were doing. The rider swinging the torch did not appear to be making any serious attempt to attack the ranch. The others hung back, the torch lighting up the scene and their horses fiddlefooting nervously as the hooded men milled around the man on the ground. Then one gave a rebel yell and sent his horse leaping forward. He swung back his torch ready to throw it.

'Drop it!' Red shouted a warning.

Flame spurted from behind the man, the bullet slapping into the wall of the house near Red. That was all the young Texan needed. His right hand Colt boomed loud, throwing flame at the leading man. The torch flew off at a tangent as the rider took lead, reeling in his saddle. From the other hooded men sounded fast shots, flame stabbing the dark and lacing at the ranch. Red was a wise hand at night fighting and knew better than to be where he'd been when he fired his shot. He slid to one side, crouching and hoping the porch furniture broke up his outline and made him a poorer target. He knew Doc was going to the other side and could guess just what Waco was doing.

Mary Anne stood by the open door. She was unable to tell what was happening and Red's shot made her start back. She felt a hand catch her arm and shove her roughly back into the house, hearing Waco snap, 'Keep in there, Rusty gal.'

With the girl taken care of Waco flung himself from the porch, landing on the ground with a gun in either hand, and saw the spurt of shots coming in a roaring answer to Red's Colt greeting. In the light of the torch he saw a stocky man directing operations. Waco knew the best way to handle any group was to down the leader. His Colt came up and lined, crashing, and as it crashed so Waco rolled sideways. He saw the man he'd aimed at clutch his right shoulder, swing his horse and yell an order.

Red's victim was down and from all around sounded the sporadic crash of shots as the men took a hand. They were shooting fast but with little effect that Red could see. The hooded men were turning now but the swaying, wounded man shouted something and they brought their horses around, shooting fast. Two of their number swung down from their horses while the rest kept up a fast covering fire. They dragged Red's victim up and shoved him across the saddle of a horse. As they ran by the man one of their party shot to their own horses and mounted again, riding off into the blackness.

'Anybody hit?' Waco called, liking the way the ranch crew held their fire until Red opened the ball. It showed they could be relied on not to spook if it came to trouble.

From the various places where they'd taken up fighting positions the answers came back. Everyone appeared to be all right. Red Blaze was moving forward, gun in hand as he stepped from the porch. He could see other shapes moving and called, 'Stop down, all of you. One target's enough at a time. More'n enough if I'm the target.'

For all the levity in his tones Red was moving like a trained lawman. The first thing he did was kick the ivory-butted Colt from where it lay by the fallen man, having slid out of his waistband. That gun was a deadly danger to Red. It was a simple precaution to remove it and the temptation it offered if the man were shamming. Then Red saw the hole in the centre of the man's back and knew there was no trickery here. That man was dead, dead as he could be when two hundred and fifty-five grains of .45 lead smashed through his spine and into his body. There was little or no blood seeping through the hole and on to the coat as yet, but Red knew this man was dead.

'Doc, come over here.' Red straightened up and thrust his gun into his waistband.

Doc advanced fast, gun in hand and ready for action. He joined Red, looking down at the body, then shoved his gun into Red's hand, bent down and rolled the body over. The clothes were not the sort a cowhand would be wearing: an old, crumpled, sober black suit, a collarless shirt, white and not too clean, and fastened at the neck by an inexpensive stud. His boots were heavy, square-toed and low-heeled; no cowhand would ever wear such boots for he would never willingly perform any task which did not entail sitting the back of a horse.

Waco turned back into the house and returned his guns to the holsters then gave Mary Anne his attention. Lee Chan came out of the kitchen with a lamp in his hand, illuminating the scene. The girl was standing flattened back against the wall but there was both anger and annoyance in her face.

'Had fun?' There was a grim note in her voice.

'Why sure,' Waco agreed, grinning.

'Good. Listen to me now, lil brother. I'm the big one in this family. Next time there's some shooting don't you go shoving me back into the house like I was some twittering, blushing Eastern biddy. You long . . .'

'Sure honey.' Waco grinned still. Ole Rusty gal hadn't changed one little bit. She was still pawing the ground and bellowing if she wasn't allowed to take her full share in anything that came up. 'Let me have the lamp, Lee. I want to go out there.'

Taking the lamp, Waco left the room, the girl following and telling him just what she thought of him, his friends, their friends and anyone who was even distantly associated with him. They crossed to where the cowhands were gathered around the body. Waco forced by them and held the lamp, looking down. Mary Anne was by his side, her face just a shade pallid as she looked at the first man she'd ever seen dead by violence.

'Did you kill him, Red?' she asked.

'Not unless my bullet went round the back and in him,' Red replied. 'It was one of his bunkies shot him.'

35

'Why'd he do that?' Mary Anne asked, then realised she'd let her tongue slip again.

'Maybe they play it different up this way,' Red replied, winking at Waco. 'Each side shoots their own men, saves bullets that way.'

Waco was not in the mood for levity right now. His brain was working fast, turning over every detail of what he'd seen out there. He was never willing to accept anything at its face value but always delved deeper, seeking out the inner whys and wherefores. He bent forward and pulled the hood from the dead man's head. In the light of the lamp a thin face showed. It was a face twisted in agony and Waco looked up at the surrounding men. 'Any of you know him?'

Larry leaned forward, examining the face closer. 'Sure I know him. It's Ben Silver. His paw's one of the nesters across the river. Kind of a preacher. But what's his boy doing riding with a bunch like that. I never even saw him pack a gun.'

'He was this time,' Red remarked, picking up the Colt Silver dropped when he came off the horse.

'Tote the body down to the barn for the night, Larry.' Waco spoke up. 'He been drinking, Doc?'

'Why sure. Smells like a moonshine still.' Doc straightened up. 'You on to something, boy?'

'Just thinking.' Waco lifted one of the dead hands, looking at it in the light of the lamp. He let the hand fall loose and nodded to Larry who, with three more of the cowhands, lifted the body and carried it off towards the barn.

They gathered in the cookshack again and Waco laid the revolver on the table and the hood by it. The rest of the ranch crew came in soon after he'd done it. Waco was looking thoughtful. He gripped the girl's hand in his and shoved her gently into a chair. Lee Chan brought coffee in, pouring Mary Anne a cup then standing back.

'You ever had trouble with the nesters before, Larry?' Waco asked.

'Nope, not more'n the occasional fist fight in town. Don't get on bad with them most times. Never see much of Ben Silver. He don't go to the saloon like the others do. Told you, his paw's a kind of preacher. Real strong against sin of all kinds.'

'Only thing not being sin is breathing, way he sees it,' another cowhand put in. 'Always on about saloons. Never thought to see his boy there drunk.'

'Or with a gun. Never thought his pappy gave him enough money to buy one.'

'He didn't buy this gun.'

All eyes went to Waco. The young man was holding the gun, turning the chamber and emptying it. Mary Anne sniffed. 'I suppose he told you?'

'Doesn't have to.' Waco held the revolver in his palm, hefting it and feeling the balance. 'This here's a real fast man's gun.'

'Are you just guessing, boy?' There was pride in Mary Anne's voice. She was satisfied with the way her little brother was growing up.

'Nope. The inside of the gun's been worked on. The safety notches on the hammer filed out. Look at the hammer spur here, the checking's been filed smooth. The gun's been used by a real fast man and that *hombre* in the barn isn't a fast gun. I looked at his hands, they've seen too much rough work for them to belong to a fast gun. This isn't his gun at all.'

Mary Anne looked at the Colt. To her eyes it was no different from any other. Waco held the smooth, hand-fitting butt in his grip and held it out to her. The ivory grips were smooth and the gun itself was made in the deep blued, best citizen's finish. She could see it was a gun which cost money and which had been well cared for. Then she saw the rough checking which usually tipped the hammer spur was filed down smooth. It was a trick she'd heard her brothers talk of, allowing for faster firing of the gun. It was not a thing a man did unless he was good with a gun. She watched as Waco drew the hammer back under his thumb. She could see the ease with which it worked, ease which made all the difference between life and death in a down grab and shoot affair.

'You seem real sure, boy.'

'I'm sure enough. I'd say this was one of a brace, could be wrong though.' With that he held the gun close to the lamp, turning it over and looking at the ivory grip. 'Man's worn it at his left side most all the time. The left grip shows just a shade more weathering than the right. You have to look real close to make it out. But it's there if you look.'

Mary Anne accepted the gun and looked down at the grips. In the light of the lamp she could make out, faintly but there all the same, that the left-side grip showed the faintest darkening. Waco asked Doc to fetch along his gun and when the slim man returned held out the ivory-handled Peacemaker for her to look at. She saw the darkening on the right side and knew Waco was right. The gun Silver had carried must have been regularly in the holster at the left side. Doc thrust his own gun away and the girl asked, 'Know anything more about it?'

'Don't know a thing about it at all. Just guessing.'

'Guess some more then,' she went on.

'Waal, I'd say it was one of a brace. It's been worked on, grip altered. I'll bet that some place there's a gun that's the mate to this one. Some place real close.'

The girl was silent for a moment, thinking over what he'd said. Red Blaze was whistling, watching Waco with the tolerant air of an elder brother watching a creditable performance by a younger. He asked, 'Are there many two-gun toting gents hereabouts, Larry?'

'A few. Two more rode in tonight.'

'Apart from us,' Red answered.

'There's a few hang around town, work for Brarsand as either table men or dealers. He's got Cholla Jocelyn, allows to be real good with a gun. Then there's Dave Tull, he *is* good. You heard of him?'

'Some,' Waco agreed. 'They say he's tolerable fast.'

'Well, he works for Brarsand, boss dealer. There's a few more of them all fair to good.'

'How many of them have a brace of ivory-handled guns though?' Red inquired.

'Tull, two or three of the others.'

'You know, this Brarsand sounds like a real important man,' Waco remarked. 'He a rancher?'

'Runs a saloon in Whittle and hires him good guns like Tull

to handle the tables. Or has Whittle grown up some since I was last there?'

'Sure it's grown. There's three more houses at least now.'

'And this gent runs a saloon there, gets him enough trade to keep all them many men going?' Waco sounded puzzled.

'Shucks, there's our crew, Wilmont's and the other two spreads. Then there's the nester families on the other side of the river,' Larry objected. 'They must take in a fair piece of money.'

'Not enough to pay for a big staff, for the likker and the upkeep of the place, if it's anything like.'

'Anything like.' Larry's pride in Whittle rose to the fore. 'I tell you, Waco, that place is as good as the best I've ever seen. Why I bet there ain't another small town like Whittle got such a place.'

'That's what I mean. Whittle isn't a big place at all. Now you allow there's a real fine saloon in town. You've got me all interested now, Larry.'

Mary Anne chuckled. She'd been thinking the same thing all the time, wondering how Brarsand managed to make a big, fine-looking saloon pay in such a small place. Even if all the cowhands spent all their pay over the bar every month it would hardly do more than meet the payroll of the saloon's hired help and cover the cost of upkeep. She couldn't see how the place could pay or, with bigger, more prosperous towns growing up all over Texas, why Brarsand chose Whittle to build.

'Did you get any of them?' Larry asked. 'I thought I saw one go down when you started shooting.'

'Red got one and I put a bullet into another's shoulder,' Waco replied. 'But they toted him off with them.'

'Pity. We might have recognised him.'

'That's why they toted him off.' Larry made the obvious remark.

'Then why did they leave the other one?'

Once more all attention came to Waco as he spoke. Red could see the young man was thinking out the reasons behind the actions again. Waco was like that; he was never content

39

unless he was delving into anything which was a little out of the ordinary.

'Maybe didn't have time to tote him along with them.' Larry and the other cowhands were more willing to go for the obvious and easy answer. 'Them nesters are . . .'

'There was only one nester riding and they left him dead. The rest of them, even if they weren't cowhands, rode better'n most any nester I ever saw,' Waco answered. 'They knew at least some of you boys would recognise Ben Silver and they still left him. Yet they toted off the other man we downed. In fact they went by Silver's body to get that one and under fire at that.'

'What do you make of it then?' Mary Anne wanted to know.

'You told me about what happened in town. Looks like somebody wants you out of the way, Rusty gal. This try tonight was aimed to scare you off, or stir up trouble between you and the nesters. Either way you'd likely give up the spread. The boy's wouldn't want to follow a woman and with a range war brewing they'd likely want to be getting out of it. You'd be left without a crew, Rusty gal. Then you'd have to sell out.'

'That means Brarsand!' Mary Anne snapped the words.

'He's one, could be any of a dozen others. Don't you go pawing earth, gal. Who's town law now?'

It was Larry who answered. 'Mean cuss called Talbot. Got him elected on the last time. Reckon the nester vote swung him in, there being some talk going round that Lafe Sanger was too old for the job.'

'Lafe's the best Town Marshal Whittle ever had,' Mary Anne snorted. 'Too old for the job indeed!'

'Thing being how's Talbot stand with you boys,' Waco interrupted Mary Anne's angry speech.

'Mean cuss, like I said. Don't take to cowhands at all. Real nester lover.'

Waco grinned. He knew that Larry, as a cowhand, disliked the man for some reason. It could be a valid one or it could be that Talbot's ideas of fun did not run to cowhand rowdiness.

40

This matter here at the ranch did not come under the province of the town marshal for it happened well beyond city limits. However, Waco always tried to stay friendly and do things right by the town law. The killing of the nester was a matter for the county sheriff's office and they should be informed unless there was a deputy sheriff in town. The town marshal's duties were concerned with the town itself and out beyond the town limits he held no jurisdiction.

'Who's County Sheriff?' he inquired.

'Vince Cole. Real nice gent from all I've seen. Don't come down this way often.' Larry was acting as spokesman for the ranch crew.

'He got a deputy in town?'

'Ole Lafe Sanger does most of the deputising for him up this end of the county. Ain't often much to do though.'

'Then it's old Lafe who'll be doing the investigation here.' Waco was relieved. Sanger was an old friend and would be fair in his judgment of the situation. There was more, far more, to this raid than first met the eye.

He laid the gun on the table and came to his feet. 'Bring a lamp along, Red. I want to go and take a look out there.'

Red knew full well Waco's skill in the reading of sign. The Ysabel Kid was a masterhand at the reading and following of sign and in Waco the Kid found an apt pupil. If there was any sign at all out there Waco would find it.

The rest of the ranch crew followed Waco and Red out, staying by the side of the house and watching as the two young men went to where the burned-out torches lay, showing the exact place of the raid. By light of the lamp Waco examined the churned ground, going over it with care. He was nearly sure that there would be no chance at all of finding anything to help him. The ground was too hard, too churned up by the hooves of not only the raiders' mounts but by the remuda of the ranch too. He knew his guessing was correct for all of that. The men who'd ridden this way were not nesters. He knew some nesters could ride well, but not with the easy grace those men showed. Ben Silver was drunk, that was plain to see. The other men were not. Waco was almost sure he could lay down

41

the full idea behind this raid but he did not aim to show his suspicions until he was sure of them.

'Rusty gal,' he said, as he and Red walked back to the others, 'We'll tote that *hombre* into town tomorrow. I want the hood put back on again. We'll make like we did not look to see who it was. I'm going to see Doc Smethers when we hit town.'

'Why?'

'Red wounded one. He's going to need some treatment. If he goes to the doctor we'll know who he is. Doc Smethers wouldn't be scared of any cheap gunny and he'll tell us. Then we can start to make a move.'

'All right. I'll let you handle it. See what sort of a mess you get us in.' Mary Anne ruffled Waco's hair. 'What do you want us to do?'

'We'll all go in to town tomorrow. All the crew. I want to show whoever's causing the trouble you've got a crew that'll stand by you.'

The girl nodded. She could see Waco was capable of handling her affairs. She wondered at the change in him. When he'd left home she was sure he'd end up as another Wes Hardin. The finished product pleased her. It would have amazed her if she'd seen him in the days when he rode for Clay Allison. Then Waco was a sullen, truculent youngster with an edgy temper and readiness to fight in his heart. The change in him since joining up with the Rio Hondo gun wizard, Dusty Fog, was amazing. His intimate friends noticed it far more than did the girl.

'Say, Mary Anne.' The girl turned and found Larry standing by her side. 'We're sorry about the way we acted when you first came in the bunkhouse. We're cowhands, not gunfighters but we're ready to stick by you now.'

'I know that.' The girl smiled back at the young cowhand. She made sure Waco was not near enough to hear, or his two friends. 'Waco's a real good man to follow and the other two are almost as good. We'll make out.'

'Why sure.' Larry went into consultation with the others then turned to the girl. 'Ole Waco ought to be talked out of dumping you in the water-trough. We have to wash in that water.'

Mary Anne was not slow on the uptake, she smiled back at the circle of faces around her. 'Yeah, he should at that.'

Waco, all unsuspecting, was standing discussing the plans for the ride into town on the following day with Red and Doc. He paid no attention to the ranch crew and the girl as they gathered around him. Then the girl gave a yell and they hurled forward. Waco was hit by a flying wedge of bodies. There was a wild and hectic struggle in which Red and Doc lent a willing hand. Bucking, struggling, held by arms and legs Waco was lifted and carried to the water-trough. The splash as he went in was like music to Mary Anne's ears.

CHAPTER FIVE

A NEAR FATAL MISTAKE

THE five men pitching horseshoes behind the livery barn turned as they heard the sound of hooves. They studied the rider, seeing a tall, slim and studious looking young man, who sat his limping black stallion with easy grace. They also noted that he wore an ivory-butted gun in a fast man's rig, trigger-guard left clear for the easy insertion of the trigger-finger. He brought the horse to a halt, swung down and lashed the pigging thong of his holster, then bent and lifted the black horse's foot and looked at the loose shoe on it.

One of the horseshoe pitchers grinned at the others and winked. He was a tall man, handsome and dressed in the style of a range dandy, buckskin shirt with long fringes, tight-legged trousers carefully tucked into his shining boots. Around his waist was a gunbelt supporting a brace of pearl-handled Colts, their butts flaring handily to his grip. His eyes took in this studious-looking young man, who was acting, or trying to act, like a big, fierce gunman. Swinging from the others this big man stepped forward towards the newcomer.

'You looking for somebody, bub?'

Doc Leroy turned and looked the gunman over with cool contempt, every working cowhand held for a man who lived by selling his guns to the highest bidder.

'Man'd say you were right.'

'Who?'

'The gent who owns the forge there. Likely it's not you though.'

'You working hereabouts, bub?'

One of the other men stood waiting for the dandy to take

his throw with the horseshoes. 'Leave him be, Cholla. Come over here and take your toss.'

Cholla Jocelyn grinned and shook his head. He was an arrant bully with gunspeed to back it up, and picking on a mild-looking pale-faced dude like this was always good fun. 'I said who do you work for?' Jocelyn held his voice hard.

'S.S.C.,' Doc answered mildly.

There was an instant change among the men. They let the horseshoes fall and moved forward to flank their friend. Doc knew he'd made him a mistake but it was one he could soon correct.

'Work for the S.S.C. do you?' Jocelyn sneered the words out. 'Now that's a real unlucky spread to work for. Man'd do better if he just got on his hoss and rode out, got clear of it.'

'That the truth?' Doc sounded interested in a polite way.

'The living truth, boy. So you can just start in by handing me that fancy-looking gun.'

'This gun?' Doc's attitude suggested he was not even sure if he was wearing a gun or not. 'Why, I couldn't rightly do that, suh. See, I'm buying it on time and it still isn't paid for.'

Cholla Jocelyn grinned and winked at the other men who stood by him. They were standing here more with the expectation of having a good laugh than with any thought of their assistance being needed. That was the rig of a real fast gunman, but this pallid-faced youngster could not be one. Only one of them was in the least worried. He was thinking of another pallid, inoffensive-looking man who talked like this one, with a sleepy southern drawl. That one was Doctor John H. Holliday, the deadly dentist of Dodge City.

Jocelyn did not know the notorious Doc Holliday and would not have taken this young man for him anyway. He held out a hand and snapped out: 'All right, hand it over.'

'If I don't?' There was a slightly different sound in Doc's voice now, and a slight difference in the way he stood.

'I'll just take it from you, bub.'

'Oh!' Doc answered gently.

Jocelyn moved forward, hand reaching out. Doc Leroy's thin, almost boneless-looking hand made a sight-defying flip

45

and the sun caught the glint on the four and three quarter inch blue barrel of his Colt. The gun was clear, lined, the hammer drawn back under a skilled thumb. The gunmen froze, all of them. Jocelyn halted with his right foot raised from the ground and hands still half reaching out, looking like a rabbit mesmerised by a snake. The dandy gulped. That draw was as fast as he'd ever seen and he'd seen fast men. Here was no pasty-faced dude dressed up in range clothes. This was the real, full growed and ready for stud thing.

'You going to take it right now?' Doc's voice was still the same but there was mocking irony in it. 'The name, *bub*, if you're interested, is Marvin Elldridge Leroy. Better known under the sobriquet of Doc.'

'Doc Leroy of the Wedge?' Jocelyn gulped the words out.

'Once, now permanently riding for the O.D. Connected and temporarily on loan to the S.S.C.' Doc watched the men, knowing they were well aware of his reputation. 'Although you seem all fired set to have me leave the S.S.C. You still wanting my gun, *bub*?'

Jocelyn gulped. The gun was back in leather again, gone back in that same flickering, lightning-fast move. The thin hand lifted and once more he looked as he did when he first rode in. There was one slight difference though. They knew how good with a gun he was. Jocelyn stood very still. He knew the other men would back his play to the last bullet, that gave him no comfort at all. There were fast men here, one at least he would say was faster than himself. But not one of them, nor any other man Brarsand hired, could face Doc Leroy's speed and walk away from the fight. There were five of them here, more than any one man could handle and live to boast of it. If they called the play that way Doc Leroy was a dead man, but before he died he would get at least two of them and probably three. They would kill Doc but the chances of survival were no more than two to one. In Jocelyn's case the odds were even lower. He knew when Doc Leroy drew, the first shot would end Cholla Jocelyn's life.

'Doc, can't you go no place without getting into trouble?'

The voice was an easy southern drawl, a cheerful sounding

'Not yet.' Waco's voice was flat and even as a crowd started to gather. 'We brought a body in.'

'Body?' The marshal's narrow eyes appeared to get even more so. 'What body's that?'

'Under the tarp in the back.' Red jerked his hand towards the wagon where Mary sat by Lee Chan. 'Take a look at him.'

'Just who might you be?' The marshal made no move to go and see the body, but stood looking them over. He could read the signs and knew that here was a real hard trio, gunhardy and dangerous to tangle with.

'We ride for the S.S.C.' Red's quick temper started to pop up at this breach of Western etiquette. 'Miss Catlan's ranch. Who are *you*?'

'Name's Talbot. Lyge Talbot. Town Marshal here.' Shoving back the side of his coat, Talbot showed his badge more plainly. 'Like I just——'

'You don't seem interested in the body back there, mister. You know who he is, or something?'

Talbot stiffened as Waco spoke. There was a fair-sized crowd gathering now, townspeople and nesters from the look of them. Waco was looking at the crowd. He saw a white-haired, thin and miserable looking old man wearing a sober black suit standing with a smaller, plump and cheery-looking nester. His eyes next went to the tall, tow-haired youngster who was standing by these two. There was worry and fear in this young man's eyes. Next his eyes went to three men who stood just clear of the crowd. Three hard-faced, hard-eyed men wearing range clothes, two of them with low-tied guns. The kid, a stocky man of medium size, better dressed than the other two, was not wearing a gunbelt. Instead, an ivory-handled Colt was thrust into his waistband, pointing towards the left. The reason for this was plain, his right arm was held in a sling.

Talbot was watching Waco, reading the signs right. It was something he'd not seen since he worked with the Earps in Dodge City as one of the noble, fearless Kansas law and order group. There he'd seen men like this youngster. Texas men, men whose names were legends. Clay Allison, Dusty Fog, Ben Thompson, King Fisher, Wes Hardin, all of them had the

49

same look as this soft-talking boy. It was the look of a man supremely confident in his skill with a gun. Since taking over as town law here Talbot gained a reputation for being tough. He wore the halo of the Kansas trailend town law proudly. The young cowhands here were not gunfighters and he'd never been called on to prove himself. Now he knew there were three men in town who were no respecters of Kansas lawmen.

With this in mind he walked to the rear of the wagon and pulled the tarpaulin from the shape which lay beneath it, looked down and then up at Waco. 'He's got a hood on.'

'Now me, I thought it was a beard,' Red scoffed.

'You make another remark like that and I'll bend a gunbarrel over your head.'

For a threat or a bluff this remark fell singularly flat. Red Balze grinned savagely, his hands stayed at his sides, the palms turned slightly out, fingers spread and ready to lift his guns clear of leather. 'That so?' he asked. 'Any time you think you can, whup ahead and start into doing it.'

Talbot backed down, climbed down faster than he liked doing. He knew that his ten-gauge shotgun did not scare this freckle-faced heller any more than it scared the blond boy. He knew he must act fast, get this over with before he lost any more face. He reached out a hand, drawing the hood from the head.

'My son?' The thin old nester came forward, his gnarled hands gripping the edge of the wagon. 'It's my son.'

The small nester moved forward also, looking down, his face losing its happy look and paling. He turned his eyes to Waco again and began to speak, 'What——?'

'My son. My son. You killed him.' The white-haired man stared up at Waco. 'You killed him.'

'No sir.' Waco's voice was gentle. 'Last night he was with a bunch of masked men who hit at the S.S.C. One of his pards shot him down, put a bullet in his back. They left him out there. I got one and wounded another before they went.'

The old man did not appear to be listening. He was standing rigid and staring at the body. Doc Leroy had laid it out for burial and the stiffening shape looked peaceful in death. It lay

50

face up and there was no sign of the wound. Ezra Silver licked his lips, swaying as he stood there. The other man caught his arm and supported him. Waco's eyes went first to the tow-headed boy then the three hard-faced men. He caught the glance which passed between them and saw the one with the sling shake his head and tap the butt of his gun. Waco's attention was drawn to the knot of the sling and his eyes narrowed, then dropped to the ivory-butted gun in the man's waistband.

'You reckon he was with that bunch that hit the S.S.C. and they shot him?' Talbot asked. 'Why'd they do a thing like that, if he was with them?'

'Because they wanted him dead and where we could find him,' Waco went on. 'The one I shot they toted off with them. Reckon they knew we'd recognise him.'

'They left this one and knew you'd recognise *him*,' Talbot pointed out. 'Yet they took the other one——'

'Sure. They wanted us to recognise this one. That way we start blaming the nesters. If we see the other man we know it's not the nesters, but, waal, whoever it was.'

Ezra Silver's face lifted and his voice was cracked as he said, 'My son is dead. Struck down in his prime and without a chance. He never even carried a gun.'

'He carried one last night,' Red held down his usually quick temper for he knew the man was feeling the loss of his son. 'That one.'

'Real fine-looking gun for a poor nester to be carrying.' Talbot picked the gun up and examined it with exaggerated attention. 'Your boy buy that gun, Ezra?'

'He never owned a gun at all.' Silver's face was haggard and the other nester supported him.

'That's right, he didn't own the gun.' Waco spoke evenly. 'Red said he was carrying one. He carried the gun but he didn't own it. He'd been drinking some, too.'

'That's a lie!' Silver straightened, shaking a fist in front of Waco's eyes. 'My boy never touched the drink of the devil. You must have taken him out to your ranch, poured whisky on him and shot him.'

Red caught Waco's arm, holding him as the young man

started forward. 'Easy boy!'

The cowhands growled out angrily and Talbot hefted his shotgun in a threatening manner. Lafe Sanger's voice cut through as he forced his way through the crowd. 'Hold hard now, Ezra. Mary Anne Catlan wouldn't back no play like that. Anyways, I'm deputy sheriff and this comes under my balliwick, not Talbot's.'

Talbot snarled something under his breath. He'd hoped for the richer pickings of deputy sheriff but the County Sheriff was adamant in his decision to leave Lafe Sanger as deputy for the Whittle area.

'All right, Lafe. Only wanted to make sure these cowhands don't start hoorawing the town. We ain't having that sort of thing here and I don't aim to.'

'Mister, this isn't Kansas. You aren't Wyatt Earp and we're not a trailcrew just paid off.' Waco spoke in a flat even tone. 'We came to town to bring this gent's son and to report that raid to the County Law. We brought the crew because we didn't know if the same bunch would be waiting for us. Another thing you might remember as Town Marshal, it's cowhands who bring the money into town, we pay your salary, friend. You're a public servant. Wouldn't you say that was right, Lafe?'

Lafe Sanger nodded. 'Why sure.'

'Then you go get me a glass of water, friend.'

Talbot opened his mouth to make some angry statement but there was something in Waco's eyes which made him pause. The young Texan was throwing out a warning in those mocking words. If Talbot pushed this matter any more there would be shooting and that shotgun was not so fast or good in a tight spot against a real fast gun. That Texas boy was a real fast gun, it showed in every line of his lithe, powerful frame.

'Now hold it all of you.' Lafe Sanger pushed forward, hand resting on the butt of his old Leech and Rigdon revolver. 'Ezra we all respects your loss but there ain't no call for you accusing Mary Anne's crew of what you did. Was your boy in town last night?'

'He came to town,' the old man's face was working. 'But he

52

never took a drink in his life, nor did he ever wear a gun.'

Once more Waco's attention was taken by the three gun-hung men and the nester boy. The boy's face was pale and he appeared to be troubled by something. Then once more Waco's eyes went to the knot of the sling and he remembered something Doc Leroy taught him about the way to put on a sling. Waco knew that there was something between the three gunmen and that boy. He was never one to let a chance slip by. The three men were turning to walk away and Waco stepped forward from the others, jerking his head in a signal which brought Doc and Red after him. They did not know what was wrong here but they were ready to back his play.

'Hurt your arm, friend?' Waco's voice, soft and caressing as it brought the men to a halt.

All three men turned, fanning out slightly, the one with the sling nodded his head. 'Fell off my hoss, landed on it.'

'That's real unlucky, falling off your horse,' Waco answered; the two men turned as if to walk away. 'Don't go yet, friend. You want to take care of things like that. Has Doctor Smethers seen it?'

'Why sure. He fixed it up for me.' The man did not turn fully round although the other two did.

'Might be as well let Lafe there take a look, too.'

'Meaning?' The man's voice dropped slightly.

'I wounded one man last night. Hit him in the right shoulder.'

'You're asking for trouble, boy.' The gunman at the right spoke up, hand lifting over his gunbutt. 'You tend to your own business or you'll be buying a tolerable heap of grief.'

The lethargy left Waco now, his voice suddenly that of a suspicious lawman questioning a suspect. 'I want to see that wound.'

'All right, boy. All right. Not any trouble at all.' The man lifted his left hand towards the knot of the sling.

'Take 'em!' The man at the right hand dipped down towards the butt of his gun.

Doc Leroy's right hand flickered and the gun was in it, ahead of the other man. The gun rocked back in his hand, throwing a shot into the body of the man, knocking him off his feet before his gun was even clear of leather. Waco's hands were going down as Doc made his move. Two shots sounded as one. He felt the hot breath of the bullet as it passed his cheek. The bullet missed and in no way put Waco off his shot. He'd made a near fatal mistake in his judgment of the man, meaning to wing him. Now there was no time, this was a real fast gun and a man could not take chances with such. His gun roared and the bullet kicked into the centre of the man's chest, staggering him, and he went down after Doc Leroy's victim.

Red Blaze never thought of himself as being a fast man with a gun. It took him all of a second to draw and shoot. The man he was up against was not good either and must have panicked at the way his two friends died. His gun was lifting clear when Red's hand twisted palm out, lifting the long-barrelled Cavalry Colt from the holster a fast done cavalry twist. The seven and a half inch barrel kicked up as flame tore from the muzzle and the man reeled under the impact of the bullet which caught him high in his shoulder. He went backwards, hit the hitching rail and hung there trying to raise the gun. Talbot yelled out something and brought up the shotgun, firing. The gunman was slammed backwards, caught by nine buckshot, his gun dropped and he followed it down.

'What the hell?' Red swung around, his face angry.

'Don't you know more'n stop shooting when a man's got a gun in his hand?' Talbot answered. 'He could have killed you.'

'Yeah.' Red's growl was deep. Talbot was right in one way. It was a prime rule for a lawman to keep on shooting when a man he'd wounded still had a gun and was willing to use it. Talbot might have been acting in good faith or there might have been a more sinister motive. The man was now dead. He might have been taken alive and able to talk.

Waco went forward with his gun held ready and rolled his victim over on to his back. There was no need for caution now. The man was dead but it was close, very close. There'd been no time for fancy shooting when dealing with a man like that. He was one of the topguns, the speed he brought the gun from his waistband and with his left hand showed it. For once in his life Waco had made the near fatal mistake in judging another man's gunspeed.

He bent down, holstering his gun and taking out a knife. Cutting away the sling below the knot he slit open the shirt and opened up the bandaging around the man's shoulder. He straightened up and pointed down to the hole.

'This's one of the men who rode on the raid last night. The other two must have been with him. What's his name?'

'That's Dave Tull. Works for Mr. Brarsand,' Sanger answered.

Waco swung around and saw both Brarsand and Della Christine in the crowd although he did not know them. 'Where do I find this Mr. Brarsand?' he asked grimly.

CHAPTER SIX

A LETTER FROM MOLLY

'You're looking at him, boy.' Brarsand stepped forward, his eyes taking in every detail of Waco's dress and appearance.

'He your man?'

'He worked for me. I fired him a couple of days back. Della found he was rigging the roulette wheel.'

Waco glanced at the saloon girl, noting the swollen, blackened eye and the fact that lipstick could not hide the swollen mouth. He wondered how she'd gained the battle-marks. Della did not give him a chance to find out, she nodded in agreement to what Brarsand said. 'Sure, we caught him and the boss fired him.'

'What's he been doing since then?' Waco asked.

'Hanging around town. What's he been doing?'

'He led a raid on the S.S.C., Mr. Brarsand. Killed the old gent's boy, either him or one of the other of the bunch did.'

'You're sure he was one of them?' Brarsand asked, never taking his eyes from Waco's face.

'Near enough sure. I hit one in the shoulder, just like he's been hit. Then he allowed he'd seen the doctor and had the wound fitted up but I knew he was lying. No doctor put that sling on.'

'How'd you know that?' Talbot growled. 'Looks like an ordinary sling, to me.'

'Sure look real ordinary. 'Cepting that a doctor allus fastens a reef knot. They're taught to do it that way, makes the knot ride easier on the shoulder. Ask Doc Leroy here, he'll tell you.'

' 'Sides Doctor Smethers went out to the Jones' place to see Mrs. Jones having a baby.' Lafe Sanger spoke up. 'Went yesterday and hasn't been back yet.'

Waco remembered what he'd heard about Dave Tull and picked up the gun which lay by the man's side. It was a real fine Colt, costly and showed sign of having had the mechanism worked on for extra speed. It was the sort of gun a real good man would tote. Then Waco looked down at the grips, holding them to the light. The right side grip showed just that slight discolouring which told him why he was still alive. That gun was slightly different in grip from the other. It was only the slightest variation, but in the hands of a master would make all the difference.

It was that slight difference, undetectable except to the man who owned the gun, which saved Waco's life. Tull was used to handling the gun in his right hand, changing it to the left threw him off that vital split-second. His using that gun meant only one thing. Waco took up the gun which Ben Silver had carried, hefting it and the other in his palm. Although he was not used to the guns he could tell they'd been balanced one against the other. This was the second of Tull's guns, the one he'd always used in his left hand.

'This's Tull's other gun. He left off his gunbelt because he'd look real strange walking around town with an empty holster at his left side. He must have given the boy the other gun when they got near to the S.S.C.'

'It happened for the best then. I think you might be right about them.' Brarsand saved Talbot answering this for which the town marshal was pleased. He owed his post here in town to the good offices of Brarsand and did not want to jeopardise his chances by taking the wrong sort of attitude. Brarsand stepped to the old man and patted his shoulder. 'I'm sorry about this, Ezra. Your boy came in the saloon last night but I made him leave. I didn't want to offend you any by serving him. I don't know where he went after that. It might have been to the Hood City Saloon.'

'It warn't,' Lafe answered. 'I was there all night. Saw him once but he never came in. He was with your boy, Wilben.'

'Not me, Mr. Sanger,' the tow-headed boy spoke hurriedly, his face pale as he stared down at the three bodies. 'I left him early on. I didn't see him at all after——'

'After what?' Waco snapped.

'Nothing.' The boy looked even more frightened. Turning he walked away before another word could be said to him.

Wilben watched his son with worried eyes, then gave his attention to the old man. Ezra Silver was standing with his hands still gripping the edge of the wagon, his face drawn. He still could hardly bring himself to believe his son was mixed up in such doings. Yet the boy was dead, and so were three other men.

'My boy, drinking. Riding about in a hood,' the old man's voice sounded strangled with grief. 'What devil's work was it he was about?'

'A man in likker does strange things, mister. Especially a man growed taking if for the first time. It was a real smart idea somebody had. Bring a nester along with them, leave him dead and stir up trouble between the ranchers on this side of the Ranse and the nesters on the other.' Waco's voice was gentle. 'I'm sorry it came to killing.'

Mary Anne climbed down from the wagon with Lee by her side. She was pale-faced like most of the crowd, for the town of Whittle was not used to the savage sudden death which struck on the streets from the guns of those three young Texas men. She moved alongside Waco and her voice was steady as she said, 'Leave it, boy. Mr. Silver I can't express in words how sorry we all are about your loss. Take the wagon and carry your boy home.'

Silver looked up. He did not appear to know what the girl was talking about. Wilben gripped the other man's arm gently and led him to the side of the wagon and helped him in. Climbing up into the wagon he reached for the reins and looked down at the girl. 'Thank you, Miss Catlan. I'll return the wagon as soon as I can after taking care of Ben's burying and getting Ezra settled down.'

'Stay by him, there's no rush for the wagon,' Mary Anne replied.

Wilben started the wagon forward, headed along the street. His son came from the sidewalk and climbed alongside him while Silver sat on the edge, rigid and with eyes staring ahead of him. The crowd started to break up now. Talbot and Lafe Sanger told some of the watchers to help carry the bodies to the undertaker's shop and followed them. On the street, Mary Anne stood by Waco and glanced at Della, wondering how the woman's face came to be marked up. Della was glaring her hate at the ranch girl who caused her to get a beating from Brarsand after losing him five hundred dollars. Though she hated Mary Anne, Della did not intend to resume hostilities. Brarsand was definite in his orders about it.

'You figured all that out well, young man,' Brarsand remarked. 'Bring your crew down to the Tavern and have a drink.'

'Not now, thanks. The boys are headed back to the spread right now. I'll be going with Mary Anne as soon as we've seen Colonel O'Dea.'

'Have you decided to take my offer, Miss Catlan?' Brarsand went on as the S.S.C. men followed Red back to where he'd left his horse. 'Although, with things happening as they are I wish I hadn't made it.'

'It doesn't need any thinking about. I'm not selling the S.S.C. and nothing's going to make me. Not riders or any other thing.'

'What makes you think there's someone trying to scare you out?' Brarsand was still smiling and friendly as he looked the girl over.

'What makes you think somebody isn't?' Mary Anne was just as friendly sounding. 'That try last night was aimed at scaring either me or the ranch crew. It didn't come off.'

'I can see that,' Brarsand replied truthfully.

'Mister,' Waco's voice cut in bringing the other man's attention to him. 'There's two real good reasons why Mary Anne here won't be scared out of her spread.' His hands brushed the butts of his matched Colts guns. 'I'm wearing them.'

Brarsand's eyes strayed down to the staghorn-butted guns, noting how they were worn. He knew how fast Dave Tull was

59

with a gun and this boy beat him to the shot. 'They're real strong reasons.'

'Sure. The next man who tries making a play at the S.S.C.'s going to find out how strong. We'll be seeing you, Mr. Brarsand.'

Brarsand did not reply as Waco and Mary Anne walked along the street. Then he turned and took Della's arm under his own, walking her back to the Tavern. 'That's a shrewd, smart young man. He'll take some watching. I wonder who he is. He isn't a hired gun, I'm sure of that. I thought she was the last Catlan.'

'She was.' Della was sullen and resentful still. 'Them two boys were the last of the brothers. There was a button they adopted, I've heard Sam talk about him. Boy they just called Waco, didn't know who he was or anything. Went off and rode for Clay Allison for a spell. That might be him. He's good with a gun.'

'Tell me something I don't know. Dave was better than most and two of them drew faster than he could. That pale-faced man, he's the one Jocelyn tangled with. Doc Leroy of the Wedge.'

'They're a bad bunch to tangle with. The redhead's another of them. What're we going to do now, Carl?'

'Nothing for a couple of days. O'Dea must have the letter by now. Then we can make our move and without risk, or without half the risk of trying to get rid of the S.S.C. by violent means.'

Colonel O'Dea received Mary Anne and Waco in his study. He was a tall, spare man, white haired and aristocratic looking. His face was tanned and keen, his eyes frank and honest, meeting a man without flinching. His clothes were still of the style worn by the deep south planter before the war and he looked as if he'd just stepped from a riverboat in New Orleans after a successful cotton selling trip.

'It's good to have you back, Mary Anne,' he greeted warmly, holding out a hand. 'I appear to remember you, young man.'

'This's my lil brother, Waco,' Mary Anne introduced.

'Waco?' O'Dea was puzzled for a moment, then he remembered the boy who'd ridden off at fourteen years old to see the West. 'Now I remember. You rode for Clay Allison, didn't you?'

'Sure, sir.' Waco noted the disapproval in O'Dea's voice and knew why. Clay Allison's crew were noted for their wild and rowdy behaviour and for skill with a gun. 'I'm riding for the O.D. Connected right now.'

'I see.' There was something like admiration in O'Dea's eyes for the O.D. Connected was known to be discriminating in their choice of hands. 'Sit down, sit down. Both of you. I hoped you would come in to see me today, Mary Anne. What was all that shooting I heard?'

Mary Anne explained as she sat down at the table. The Colonel did not speak, listening to all the girl told him. His eyes kept flickering towards Waco as he listened. At the end he nodded in approval. 'Not enough evidence to take to a court of law, but it was not needed the way things turned out. Now we'll get down to the other business. The S.S.C. is solvent, Mary Anne: and has never been more so. Under the terms of your father's will you as sole surviving kin inherit it——'

'But Waco's my brother,' Mary Anne objected.

'Only adopted as you both know. Not even legally adopted. I'm sorry. Mary Anne but that is how it stands. To carry on, you don't owe anyone a red cent, except for the time due to the hands. If that was all you wouldn't have a thing to worry about.'

'Is there more then?'

'Not so far, but there could be. Your water supply might be curtailed, which would ruin your land.'

'How?' Mary Anne asked. 'The Ranse River forms our main supply and from what I saw there is plenty of water in it.'

'The headwaters are on the Lazy W property.'

'They always have been. Molly Wilmont and her pappy would never interfere with them. They never have.'

O'Dea nodded, taking out a box of cigars and offering it to Waco. The young man accepted, lit the smokes and sat back, listening, knowing there was more than just casual conversation behind the Colonel's words.

'I agree with you. *They* have never interfered with the running of the water. You know of course, that since her father died last year, Molly has been living in Chicago and leaving the ranch running to her foreman, Whit Dwyer, with myself acting with power of attorney for her interests in matters which Whit could not manage?'

'I didn't know, but that figgers.' Mary Anne sounded puzzled.

'Well, she wrote and asked me to sell the ranch.'

'She did *what*?' Mary Anne came to her feet, leaning forward with both hands resting on the table top and looking down at the man.

'I received this letter only this morning.' O'Dea reached inside his coat and pulled out a letter holding it to Mary Anne.

Mary Anne took the letter, glancing at the sprawling, not over elegant writing and recognising it for what it was. She'd seen enough of Molly Wilmont's writing to recognise this now. Taking out the sheet of paper she read the short, concise and businesslike note asking Colonel O'Dea to sell the Lazy W and act in all matters dealing with the disposal of it as soon as possible. She examined the notepaper. It was from the Reed-Astoria, one of the best hotels in Chicago.

'Are you sure she wrote this letter?'

'How do you mean, girl. Am I sure?'

Mary Anne handed the letter back to O'Dea before she replied. 'I know Molly, she's been like a sister to me. Put a pen in her hand and she's away like the devil after a yearling. Molly would never write a short note like this. You'd have had five or six sheets with news and asking about folks with the business of selling the spread mixed in with it. She'd never write anything as clear and concise as this.'

O'Dea scowled at the letter, then rose and went to the door to yell for his daughter, Susan Mae. The girl came, a slender, pretty blonde about Mary Anne's age. She smiled a delighted greeting to the ranch girl but did not get a chance to greet her. O'Dea asked Susan Mae to go to her room and fetch any letters she might have from Molly Wilmont and the girl knew better than waste time when he used that tone of voice. She left and soon after came back, carrying three envelopes. The Colonel extracted the letter from the first, checking on the handwriting, then glancing at the way Molly wrote. There was eight pages of the sprawling writing and the Colonel saw straight off what made Mary Anne suspicious. Molly wrote slower than she thought, apparently. Her letter was disjointed, one moment asking about the welfare of her pet horse, then going right on to describe a dance she'd attended, then on to something of more interest.

'This looks like the same handwriting for all that.'

'Mind if I look, sir?' Waco inquired and took the letters. He crossed to the window and held them both to the light, studying the writing with care. 'I'm no expert on things like this, but I'd say it was two different hands that did this.'

'A forgery?' O'Dea's face reddened. 'By cracky, boy, if I thought it was I'd——'

'Why'd anybody want to forge a letter like this though, Colonel?' Waco cut through the hot-tempered threats.

'Well, I've power of attorney as I just told you and can handle *any* business she wishes me to. With this letter I would take up any reasonable offer which came my way.'

'Without consulting her?'

'That depends. Her letter says take the best offer I can and sell as quickly as possible. If the price was right I'd sell without worrying her any. That's the idea of having an attorney.'

Waco laid down the cigar, his face showing nothing of the way his thoughts were whirling, sorting and debating the reason for this letter. 'Unless I recollect wrong, Rusty gal, there was two watercourses to the Ranse, the one it follows and a drywash that only fills when there's a real high fall of rain in the hills. But dam the top of the Ranse and that other cut would get the water, run the Ranse dry and leave you out. If the Lazy W wanted to make the dam, that is.'

'Molly wouldn't do a thing like that.'

'It wouldn't be legal, either,' O'Dea pointed out.

'Sure, but a rock slide could do it and who could tell if that same slide was accidental or caused by dynamite?'

63

'I tell you Molly wouldn't pull any play like that, boy,' Mary Anne snapped, watching Waco's face. 'You always was slow at picking things up unless they was for eating.'

'Sure Molly wouldn't do it,' Waco agreed. 'But what if she sells out and the next owners aren't so friendly?'

'It would have complications, bad complications if the next owner was wanting to be awkward and make trouble,' O'Dea remarked. He saw his daughter was standing listening and waved her from the room. 'Is that what might be behind the letter, if it is a forgery?'

'It could be. That letter is to make you sell out when somebody comes along with a real good offer. They can afford to pay high for the Lazy W, they'll control all the water and with the Ranse run dry they can buy out the S.S.C. and the nester land cheap.'

Mary Anne paced the room. She halted by the table and her face was grim. 'I tell you Molly wouldn't sell out the Lazy W without making sure Whit and her crew were well taken care of first. It just doesn't fit Molly at all.'

'I thought that myself when I first received the letter. I checked the postmark on the letter. It was posted in Chicago all right. I wish there was some way I could talk with her.'

'That might be the answer, Colonel. I'd like to take this letter along with me when Rusty and I head for Chicago,' Waco put in.

'Well, I'm not sure it would be correct for me—head for Chicago. What do you mean, boy?'

'Molly's in Chicago, I figger she'll hear us better if we go to her than if we stand out in the street here and holler. Rusty and I'll go overland by hoss to the railhead, then take a train East. We can make better time than going by stage, night over at a couple of places along the way.'

'Hm! It might be possible, except for one small matter. Two young people like you travelling together might excite some curiosity, especially when one is a pretty and unmarried girl, the other a man.'

'Why Colonel,' Mary Anne sounded far more shocked than she felt. 'Waco's my lil brother. Anyways I think it's the best thing we can do. If Molly isn't selling and didn't write that letter we can get to her long before a letter could. If she is thinking of selling I'll bring her back here if I have to yank her all the way by the hair.'

O'Dea belonged to a more leisurely age when a young lady did not casually talk of going off on a long jaunt with a man, even if he was her adopted brother. This modern youth was beyond him and he was not at all sure he approved of it. One thing he did know, there was no stopping Mary Anne Catlan once she made up her mind. She was like her mother in that.

'I'd surely like the letter to take along, Colonel. And when you get the offer for the ranch you can safely and truthfully say you don't have a letter from her. It won't be a real, out-right lie if you say it that way. You won't have the letter.'

'You've got a real law wrangler's mind, boy,' Mary Anne scoffed. 'All filled up with tricks——' Then she stopped and her face reddened. She'd forgotten that Colonel O'Dea was also a law wrangler.

O'Dea laughed. He was used to having range people regarding his profession with suspicion. He handed over the letter with a smile playing on his lips. 'Mary Anne's nearly correct at that. You've got the right sort of mind to make a lawyer. You've got more on your mind than just easing my conscience over this.'

'I'll tell you the truth, sir. I have. Know a man in Chicago who might be able to help us. Like you say the letter was posted there, I reckon it was written there, too. If it is a forgery, it's a good one and done by a tophand. He'll likely be able to point us to a few likely ones.'

'What is he, this friend of yours. A bank robber?' Mary Anne inquired. Her little brother seemed to know the strangest people.

'Not quite. He's a Detective-Lieutenant of the Chicago Police. I met him a piece back. Helped him some and he'll likely do the same for me. I'll get a telegraph message off to him as soon as we know when our train leaves for the East, he'll meet up with us at the depot.'

'You think he can help?'

65

'Why sure, Ed's been a policeman in Chicago all his adult life and knows them all. Like I said, this kind of work here's not been done by a yearling, it's tophand stuff. There can't be more than two or three men in Chicago capable of it. If it can be done Ed'll point us to the men who wrote it. Then I'll find out why.'

'When will you leave?' O'Dea asked.

'Today, as soon as we get back to the S.S.C. I'll leave my paint with Doc and Red. He don't take to strangers and I wouldn't want to leave him in the livery barn at the railhead. We'll take a couple of speed horses and light out on them.'

'Won't be able to take much luggage, travelling like that,' Mary Anne pointed out.

'Never thought we could. We'll take just enough to last us to the railroad and then buy some more when we get there.'

'That's all right for you, boy. But I like to travel neat.'

'You always did,' Waco laughed and ruffled her hair. 'Like when you went coon hunting and lost the seat of your pants. Come on, you can pack a dress or two and tote them along in a warbag.'

Mary Anne chuckled. Her little brother might be able to think things out and figure the whys and wherefores, but he surely did not know much at all about women's clothes. Not if he thought a stylish city dress could be bundled up and wrapped in a warbag.

CHAPTER SEVEN

MARY ANNE PAYS A CALL

CHICAGO in 1879 was almost over the Great Fire which gutted and decimated most of it in '71. It was also trying to establish itself as a prosperous eastern metropolis and live down the era of rowdiness. Down by the stock yards a man could still find western style clothes. In the badlands, the slum areas which surrounded most of the business sections life was much the same, but up in the North-East, in the area they called Streeterville, the new rich made their homes, built their high-class hotels, and lived a life well clear of the rougher element of town, striving to lift their cultural level to that of New York or San Francisco.

It was into the depot of the westbound railroad that Mary Anne and Waco arrived. They'd bought clothes more suitable in the railhead town, the best money could buy for them, but Mary Anne knew she was hopelessly outmoded. Waco still retained his Stetson and high-heeled boots but wore store suit, white shirt and black string tie. From under the bottom of his coat showed the tips of his holsters, the pigging thongs fastened to his legs. He stood by the girl and looked at the milling crowd around him.

'Man, oh man. Just look at all the folks,' he said. 'Looks like ole Dodge City in the train season.'

A man came through the crowd, a man as big as Waco, and older. He wore a curly brimmed derby and brown suit, with town shoes on his feet shining as he walked. He was not a good-looking man, yet there was a rugged attraction about his face, his teeth were rather prominent and gave him a look of furtive amusement. He held out a powerful hand which Waco gripped eagerly. 'Howdy Ed,' he greeted. 'Glad to see you again.'

'Same applies, boy. I thought you might be in on the train so I came down to greet you.'

There was genuine pleasure about the meeting. Lieutenant Ed Ballinger owed Waco his life. That was in the days when he chased a gang of big city criminals down to the Rio Hondo country of Texas. It was in the Rio Hondo country Ballinger learned that Western lawmen were far from country hicks and Waco was one of the men who had shown him.

Ballinger's eyes dropped to where the tips of Waco's holster showed and a grin broke across his face. 'I knew you'd come wearing all that armament, boy. Here, you'll need this.'

Waco accepted the sheet of paper held out to him. 'What is it?'

'A firearms permit.'

'A *what*?' Waco almost shouted the last word, bringing several people to a halt.

'Firearms permit. You need one to tote a gun around here. And we don't even like folks doing it. I had the hell of a time getting it for you, even you are still a Deputy Sheriff of Rio Hondo County, so don't go shooting out the street lights.'

'Lord, what'll they think of next?' Waco sounded shocked. 'Hell, just think how we'd be if we had to get one of these things every time we wanted to go to town.'

'This isn't the West, boy. We're civilised here. So they tell me!' Ballinger glanced inquiringly at Mary Anne.

Tucking the permit into his notecase Waco introduced the girl, but did not offer to explain his business any. 'Come along to the Reed-Astoria, Ed. I'll tell you all about it when we get there.'

'All right. I've got nothing but time. Took me a day or so off when I heard you were coming. Reckoned we'd make a round of the town. I owe it to you. Don't know about it now, though. Chicago's a town full of evil temptations.'

'And I bet you was going to introduce him to most of them,' Mary Anne remarked, eyeing Ballinger grimly. 'Can't say I approve of my lil brother doing things like that. But I don't reckon that's going to stop either of you any.'

Ballinger led the way to the stand where Victorias stood ready for hire. He opened the door of one and helped the girl in, then climbed into sit next to her. Waco swung up and joined them, facing them and waiting until the coloured porter brought their one small bag. He tossed the grinning man a coin as the bag was passed to him, then the driver started his horse forward.

There was little talking done on the trip for Waco was absorbed by the sights of this, the biggest city he'd ever seen. They left the poorer section and came towards Streeterville, the streets widening and the buildings becoming more imposing all the time. Waco's attention was held by the stores, then they came to a halt before a large, stone-built establishment. Over the awning, in large black letters was the sign 'Reed-Astoria Hotel'. It was the best, most elegant place in Chicago and Waco felt a momentary panic. He knew the social graces, having learned them at the O.D. Connected, but the chances to use them were sadly lacking in the West. Yet he'd never even thought of staying at such a place as this.

'Wowee?' The words came from him as he looked at the building. 'There's nothing like this in Dodge City. I bet they make you shave before they'll have you in the barbershop.'

Mary Anne and Ballinger laughed at this. They were both watching the young man and comparing Waco in the city to Waco on the range. There he was the master of every situation, knowing the land and at home in it. Here he was a stranger, out of his depth almost. Ballinger could appreciate Waco's feelings. He'd felt the same way when the stagecoach carried him over the miles of open range into an unknown land. Then he'd been the one who was lost and Waco helped him out, Waco and the members of Ole Devil's floating outfit.

Mary Anne was used to buildings like the Reed-Astoria and led the way into the hotel. Inside she saw people looking her over and was conscious that she was not as well dressed as she would like to be, when entering a place like this. The fat desk-clerk studied her and Waco with a frown as they walked to the desk, then glanced at Ed Ballinger, nodded a greeting and turned a frigid face to the girl.

'I want two adjoining rooms.'

'You wish a room *here*, madam?'

'Miss. And I want two rooms, *here*, right now.'

The clerk gulped. He'd seen some of these Texas people before. They were inclined to get rowdy if they did not receive attention and firm handling. He hoped they would not cause a scene for there were the other guests to consider, including the Earl of Hawksden and his wife. In fact the Earl was coming now, striding along the hall, his monocle gleaming in his eye. He stopped and looked at the tall young man. The clerk gulped, hoping this rough-looking young man did not offend the Earl's susceptibilities for the British aristocrats were known for their dislike of democratic ways. The Earl was advancing now, screwing his monocle more firmly in his eye.

'Waco, you damned old hell twister. Gad! It's good to see you.'

Waco turned. For a moment he did not recognise this elegant and stylishly attired young man, then he grinned and gripped hands with a whoop of: 'Brit! What the hell are you doing in that get-up?'

The two men shook hands and Mary Anne stared at them, then at the clerk whose eyes were bulging out like two balloons. She did not know this elegant-talking dude, but apparently the clerk did, so did Ballinger from the look on his face.

'Say Mary Anne, this's Brit. We met down in Azul Rio Country when we was helping Mark's cousin.'

'Pleased to meet you.' Brit held out his hand to the girl. 'Are you Mrs. Waco?'

'Not under any circumstances. I'm his big sister.' Mary Anne turned to the clerk again. 'About those rooms?'

'There is the suite, next to mine, Jules,' Brit remarked. He could guess what was going on.

'Yes sir, my lord.' Jules grabbed up the pen and turned the register. 'Of course, sir. Front!' A page darted forward. 'Take this lady's bags to her room.'

'Shucks, ain't no call for that.' Waco scooped up the bag. 'I'll take it.'

'This *is* annoying.' Brit sounded exasperated. 'Gloria and I have to leave on the train tonight. If I'd known you were coming I'd have stayed on a few days. You'll have to come and see Gloria before we leave, Waco. She'd never forgive me if you didn't.'

Jules looked at the book after Mary Anne filled it in, noting the address was a Texas ranch. His eyes met Ballinger's inquiringly as the Earl of Hawksden talked to Mary Anne and Waco, Ballinger leaned forward across the desk and dropped his voice in a confidential whisper. 'You're lucky, Jules. If you'd offended them you'd have been looking for a new job. He'd likely have bought the hotel and tossed you out of it.'

Jules gulped and held his voice down. 'Are they rich, then?'

'Just about the richest in Texas. The chief asked me personally to take care of them.'

Jules' face showed his worry now. Ballinger was head of the Chicago murder division of the police and an important man in his own right. For so important a man to have been given the task of shepherding this couple must mean they were important also. Of course, many of the Texas new-rich people were likely to turn up dressed below themselves. It was just their democratic way of doing things. They were good natured, if a trifle rowdy. The Reed-Astoria was used to a certain amount of rowdiness, the amount depending on the bankroll of the person involved. The Texans were the worst, boisterous, inclined to shoot out the fittings. They were also more generous in their repayment for any damage they might cause and would give out large sums on leaving.

He handed the girl the key to the suite and waved the page forward to take them to their rooms. Mary Anne turned to the man again. 'Is Miss Molly Wilmont here?'

'No madam.' There was a respectful note in Jules' voice now. Miss Wilmont was a respected customer. 'She is attending a music afternoon at the home of her fiancé.'

'Who might he be?'

'Mr. Keith Wellington. Of the Streeterville Wellingtons.'

'Thanks.' Mary Anne followed the others.

There was not time to discuss the urgent business which brought them to Chicago yet. Brit fetched his wife, Gloria, and there was a happy reunion with inquiries about old friends. They lunched in Brit's suite and afterwards they left the Earl and his wife to get on with their packing. Gloria and Brit would have liked to stay on with Waco for a few days but business was calling them back home to New Mexico and their reservations were booked on the train. Mary Anne was more amazed at her little brother than ever. He knew the most remarkable people and appeared to have a range of friends which extended from gunfighters and Chicago policemen to a scion of the British aristocracy.

In the dining-room of their suite, which Waco described as being bigger than one hotel he'd used in Texas, they settled down to talk.

Waco was making a study of his surroundings. He grinned at the other two and took a seat in the comfortable chair. 'Man, this is really living. Ole Red Blaze never had it this good, he just wouldn't appreciate it none. Beats all I've ever seen. Even the one in El Paso. That was some place in its way. I was in bed the first night and there was a knock on the door, a voice shouted, "This is the manager, have you got a woman in there?" I said, "No," so they opened the door and threw one in.'

Ballinger laughed. 'You didn't come all the way to Chicago just to tell me windies like that, did you?'

'Nope. This here's what brought me.' Waco extracted the letter which O'Dea received and which was reputed to have been sent by Molly Wilmont, then added to it one Mary Anne produced also from Molly.

Taking the two letters Ballinger glanced at them, read both, then looked up. 'Well?'

'Real nice, aren't they?'

'Sure, lady writes a good letter. What's so interesting?'

'She only wrote one of them.'

Ballinger took up the letters again. He went to the window and held them to the light. There was no change in his facial expression at first, then he turned and there was a glint in his eyes. He was more interested in this than he let on.

'I'd near on swear they were written by the same hand. If one's a forgery, it's real good.'

'Thought that. It's why I asked you to come and meet me. I'd say no year-old beef handled the pen on that. It was written by a mossyhorn at the game, a real tophand. How many men in Chicago could handle a thing as good as this?'

Ballinger frowned. 'Right now not more than two. And I doubt if they could handle it well enough. Not this much writing. Sure, they'd do your signature so that nobody could tell the difference, but not write as much as this and address the envelope. There's not a man in all Chicago who's that good. Not now.'

Something the way Ballinger said this made Waco suspicious. The Detective Lieutenant was more than just casually interested in this forgery. There was more to it than first met the eye. Ballinger knew criminals, knew them as Waco knew the cattle business, as only a tophand could know them. He knew who'd done the writing of this letter, but there was more to it than just that.

'How about when the letter was written?' Waco asked. 'Which was afore that date there on the postmark stamp.'

'There was one man who could handle it. He was the best of them all. I never heard of a forger who could touch him. His name was Doc Pilsener.'

'Where at's this here said Doc Pilsener now?'

'That's a real good question, boy. There's only one of two places he could be and I wouldn't want to guess which he's at right now.'

'Try real hard, just for me,' Waco prompted.

'It could be heaven, although knowing old Doc's tastes on this earth I doubt it. We found him the day after this letter was posted. He was laying down in the stockyards.'

'Dead?' Mary Anne asked innocently.

'Never seen anybody deader. Shot three times in the back with a heavy calibre gun. Poor old Doc, must have mortified him being found dead down there. He was always fond of the elegant life and never went into the badlands if he could help it. Then gets killed down there, shot with a heavy calibre handgun.'

'That'll be a lot of help. There can't be more'n a couple of million .44 revolvers in the country and maybe not more'n three or four million .45's of different sorts. Unless there was more to it than that!'

'There was. We got the bullets out of him. All three of them and holding their shape. They were interesting, real interesting. I don't know if you hick lawmen know it but we've been making strides in this scientific crime detection. Got us systems of identification which are real good. We've also got a collection of bullets fired from Colt, Remington, Smith & Wesson, Merwin & Hulbert, Forehand & Wadsworth revolvers. We can compare most kinds of bullets we get with those in our files.'

'And this one was?' Waco asked, knowing there was something out of the ordinary. He was so interested that he did not make any comment on the subject of Eastern lawmen when confronted by an ordinary, everyday task which a Western lawman was accustomed.

'It wasn't any of them. So we asked around the place after we measured up the bullet. It was .450 calibre and that helped Kitteridge, the firearms dealers; helped us in the end. The gun they reckon it was fired from is made in England, a Webley R.I.C., stands for Royal Irish Constabulary. They'd one in stock and we got a bullet from it. Now all we've got to do is find a man who's got him a Webley R.I.C. revolver, was in Chicago, knew Doc Pilsener and had a good reason to kill him. It's as easy as that.'

'Like to see one of those Webley guns. I haven't ever seen one,' Waco remarked. 'Reckon we could go to that place and take a look at the gun they've got?'

'Sure, I'll take you as soon as you're ready.'

Waco paced the room for a time. Then he halted and said, 'Look, Ed. This letter here,' he indicated the forgery. 'It was written on paper from this hotel. Who can get that paper?'

'I don't know. Reckon anybody could if they wanted. Hold it for a minute and we'll find out.' Ballinger left the room and

74

returned soon after with Jules, the desk clerk. 'Jules, who can get hold of the hotel notepaper, any of the staff?'

'No sir.' Jules sounded horrified at the thought. 'The hotel stationery is not for use by any of the staff.'

'Could the hired help get hold of it, happen they wanted?' Waco inquired.

'Hardly, sir. We take care that they do not. It leads to abuses. There is no paper in the writing room downstairs. If anyone wishes to use the hotel paper they send to me and I personally deliver it. I or one of the other desk clerks, whoever is on duty. I hope nothing is wrong, Lieutenant.'

'Nothing at all, thanks, Jules. I want to have a look at the register on my way out.'

'Register?' Jules gulped. 'I trust that there is nothing wrong which might reflect on the high standard of the hotel.'

'Nothing at all, Jules. I just like reading hotel registers. It's surprising how many Smiths there are in the world.'

Jules sniffed pompously. 'Not at the Reed-Astoria.'

Waco closed the door on the slightly offended, little fat man and grinned. 'Reckon he's telling the truth. His kind live for the place they work for. I bet he counts out each sheet, just to make sure they don't fall into the wrong hands. You know what that means, Ed, don't you?'

'Sure. It means the man who got the paper stayed here.'

'Could it be Doc Pilsener?' Mary Anne asked, then shook her head. 'No, of course it couldn't. He was a crook.'

'You'd never have known it to see him. He always dressed to the height of fashion, was a real gentleman. His kind has to be. Can you see a bank clerk handing money over to a man who looks like he's fresh from cow-prodding on a cattle-train?'

'I suppose not,' the girl answered. 'It could have been him then!'

'I doubt it. Jules there knows nearly every big-timer criminal in Chicago. He wouldn't entertain the idea of having Doc Pilsener even in here.'

'Let's work the range this ways, then,' Waco spoke up. 'The man who killed Pilsener is the one who paid for this letter to be written. That means he's the one who I want as well as you,

75

Ed. He's a man who's been in Chicago and stayed on here as a guest. Likely not be under the name we know him, if we do. Is there any chance of my getting one of the bullets that killed Doc Pilsener to take back with me?'

'I reckon we could fix it. The Chief's being chased by the papers because of Pilsener's killing. It came just at a time when the Chief was saying we'd cleaned up the town. He wants the man who did the killing. I'll be able to get you one of the bullets if I tell him you're still working as a deputy sheriff. Are you?'

'Still hold the badge, although I haven't done any work for the sheriff for a piece. I want to check the bullet against a man's gun.'

'Whose gun, boy?' Mary Anne asked.

'I'm not saying yet, big sister. Hondo Fog always told me never to name a name until I was real sure. When I am, I'll name him. It might even come out I'm wrong.'

'You usually are.' Mary Anne smiled as she watched Waco.

'You think Doc Pilsener's killing is tied in with whatever brought you here, boy?' Ballinger asked. 'It's a real long shot. Doc made him some enemies in his life.'

'Sure, but it's too much of a coincidence to think one of them killed him just after he'd finished a job like this. Was there any money on him when you found him?'

'Pockets were empty, everything gone from them. I've got some pictures of his body at Headquarters. That's another way we have of working out here now. Photograph the body so we've got proof of how it lay and everything.'

'Did you search his room?' Waco asked.

'Sure. It'd been gone over real careful before we got there and there was a pile of charred-up paper in the fireplace. We didn't find anything to help us except some blood. Looks like Doc was shot there and took out to the stockyards to be dumped.'

'Looks like I'm right, too. Call it this way, Ed.' Waco's eyes were glowing with eagerness. 'This man who killed Doc hired him to write this letter. He wrote it, then tried to blackmail the other man, or get more money out of him. That was why

76

he was killed. Would that fit in with what you know of Pilsener?'

'Sure it would.' Ballinger could see the country boy in the city air was falling from Waco now there was a serious job on hand, a job the youngster was as good at as was Ballinger himself. 'Doc was always a greedy cuss.'

'Then the man killed him, he'd got what he wanted. Searched the room to make sure there was nothing to point to him. Destroyed all the papers. Then took Doc out to the stockyards and dumped him. But what I don't know is how the man would know to contact Doc in the first place.'

'I don't follow you, boy,' Mary Anne put in.

'A man like Pilsener doesn't put a note in a paper saying, "Doc Pilsener, Expert Forger, available for work",' Waco answered. 'But this man knew how to find him. Let's go take a look at the register, go to Kitteridge's and see the revolver, then along and see Molly.'

They left the room and went to the desk. Ed Ballinger turned the register, flipping the pages until he came to the date of the letter. In the three days immediately before, during and after the killing only five people had left the Reed-Astoria. A man and his wife from New York, a Mr. Bannister whom Ballinger knew, a titled Englishman going west on a hunting trip and a Mr. Jackson who was marked as a businessman from Denver. Ballinger closed the book and handed it back to Jules, then turned to Waco. 'Satisfied?'

'What's this here Mr. Jackson look like?' Waco inquired.

'Big, always well dressed. A gentleman.'

'So's Cole Younger,' Waco answered. 'Can't you do better than that, friend?'

'A rather distinguished-looking gentleman if I remember. I'm afraid I see so many people I rarely take much notice of them. He was acquainted with several members of the Streeterville Sporting Club.'

There was nothing more to be found out here so they left the hotel and took a Victoria to Kitteridge's Hardware and Sporting store. The manager of the gun department greeted Ballinger as a friend and took them to the gun showroom.

They were passing through the fishing department when Waco found something which brought him to a halt. He went to a counter and looked down at the thing which lay there. 'What's this?' he asked.

It looked like a flattened out fish, was made of two pieces of rubber shaped like the wings of a grasshopper, a metal set of fins and swivel at front and three triangle hooks attached to it. 'It's an English fishing lure called a phantom. We received a consignment of them a few months ago. They're deadly for bass fishing. We're the sole suppliers in this country.'

Waco thought of the big old bass on the Ranse River and the time people spent in trying to catch him. 'I'll take one of them,' he said.

With his purchase in his pocket he went on to the gun showroom. Here he was at home, among the smells of gun oil and fine woodwork. He was shown the Webley Royal Irish Constabulary revolver. It looked a good enough gun but the butt was not as well made as that of the Colt Peacemaker, that was the finest grip ever used on a handgun. 'Sell many of them?' he asked.

'Not too many. They're hard to get ammunition for. Don't take the normal .45 bullet, it's too long for the R.I.C.'s cylinder. We're not the sole agents, but I've given the Lieutenant a list of all we've sold.'

Waco was turning to leave when he saw a rifle on a rack. It was like a Winchester Model of '73 but looked heavier and longer. Always interested in weapons he went to the rifle. The manager followed him and, salesman at heart, said, 'This is the latest model Winchester lever action. Centennial model of 1876. Calibre .45.75. Chamber capacity is cut down to twelve shots, but the range is greatly increased.'

Waco took the rifle from the rack hefting it. It was heavier than the Model of 1873 which he was used to. However it also possessed several advantages: it was heavier and took a better bullet. His own rifle was in need of renewing and this would be just the answer. 'How much are they?'

'This model sells for forty-eight dollars.'

'I'll take it. Box of a hundred shells for it and a reloading outfit.' Waco turned to Mary Anne as he finished making his order. 'Sure wish I'd known about that bet Della was going to make about you and her. I'd have won enough to take me another hundred hulls.'

Ballinger laid down the short-barrelled Colt Lightning revolver he was looking at and came over. 'Did you say Della?'

'Sure, why?'

'Doc Pilsener used to go around with a girl called Della. A blonde, real good looking, about your size, Mary Anne.'

Waco rested the rifle on the counter again and swung to face Ballinger, his face showing his eagerness. 'What was her other name?'

'Who, Della?' Ballinger frowned for a moment. 'I'm not sure. I think it was Della Christine.'

CHAPTER EIGHT

THE S.S.C. LOSES CATTLE

RED BLAZE took command of the S.S.C. ranch without any great worry as to his ability to handle things. He'd acted as segundo of his brothers' ranch back home and helped Dusty Fog out enough to know how to handle things here. He and Doc were skilled cowhands, they'd got the backing of a good crew and even though there was a chance of trouble they were not worried.

For two days they handled the chores of the ranch, keeping the men close in and doing the chores around. Then on the third Red slung his double-girthed Texas saddle on his big claybank stallion. He called Larry and Doc and they rode out over the range looking for odd chores the other hands could take care of. It was a rule that the ranch buildings were never left unattended, there were always two of the crew to stay behind, their orders, in case of attack, or needing Red back in a hurry were to light the fire in the house sitting-room, heap it with wet grass and make plenty of smoke. The ranch crew who were on the range had their orders to return as fast as possible if the signal was sent up.

A mile from the ranch they came on a herd of some two hundred head grazing quietly down at the foot of a long slope. The cattle were in a great fold of land. There was plenty of food and water for them.

'Stock herd, in case we ever need them in a hurry. They don't move about much. Stay down there most times, the food's good and plenty of water. The boys come out this way every other day or so just to check on them and make sure they're all right.'

REPLICA GUNS...

are superb machined metal working model guns. Some are constructed from 50 component parts. Each model is made to close tolerance specifications to reproduce closely the actual size, weight and balance of the original gun. All models field-strip, *yet cannot be fired*.

COLT GOVERNMENT .45
Standard sidearm of the American Army in both World Wars.

LUGER P.08
George Luger's world renowned toggle action automatic. Standard sidearm of German Army in World War I.

SMITH & WESSON .357 SNUB MAGNUM
The most widely used sidearm of Secret Service and F.B.I. agents. Six shot, swing-out cylinder and 2″ barrel. Weight 1½ lb.

For the full range of over 25 fully working Replica Models, fast draw holsters and accessories, fill in and post this card today.

Postage will be paid by licensee

Do not affix Postage Stamp if posted in Great Britain, Channel Islands or N. Ireland.

BUSINESS REPLY SERVICE
Licence No. EA 216

REPLICA MODELS (UK) LTD
34 NORTH STREET
HAILSHAM, SUSSEX

Red nodded. He understood this. The O.D. Connected and many another ranch held the nucleus of a herd like that for use in case of a fast market being found. The herd down there, with good water and grazing were not likely to stray far. The cattle were not longhorns but whitefaces, the cattle which were fast replacing the old, ornery longhorn. It was the march of progress. The longhorn was ideally suited to open range grazing for it was half wild and could live off the land like a wild animal. The only trouble was the longhorn's beef was not up to the same high standard of the whiteface's. The whiteface cattle were easier to handle, less likely to raise hell when being shipped by rail. Their arrival was a marking of the end of the old, open-range days when a man's cattle roamed at will, were gathered in the great round-ups which often covered many hundreds of miles and involved many separate ranches.

Red was never one for dreaming of the days gone by. He lived for the day, lived full, wild and reckless like a true cowhand. Never one to be hampered by self-restraint, Red was regarded, by the people he came into contact with as the *enfant terrible*. He lived under the shadow of his more illustrious cousin, Dusty Fog. Even in the War he'd been under Dusty's shadow, as his second in command. Folks tended to treat Red as an amiable but reckless young heller. Only one man really knew his full capabilities. That man was Dusty Fog. Dusty knew that Red might act in a wild and reckless way, that he could and often did jump feet first into any fight that was going. He also knew that when once in the fight Red became as cool and capable as he usually was wild and reckless.

Right now Red was accepting his responsibilities. He was cool and would not let himself be swayed from his duties, nor would he fail in them. He turned the big claybank and rode across the range again with the other two men by his side.

'Buzzard, Red,' Doc pointed ahead. 'He's circling like he's over something and calling the rest of the boys up.'

They rode across the range making for where the buzzard was spiralling and saw what was wrong. A lone bull stood there moaning dolefully and making no attempt to avoid them as they rode nearer.

'Looks sick to me,' Larry remarked.

Red unstrapped his rope and rode nearer the bull, swinging the loop gently. He watched the big animal carefully and rode around it to flip the loop out in a hooleyann throw which landed the rope around the head and drew tight.

'He's all swelled up here, Red,' Doc announced as he rode behind the bull and looked down. He'd been almost sure of what the trouble was and this was proof.

'He's one of our best bulls. A mite old but he's still the best we've got. Going to shoot him?'

'Nope. Goodnight him.'

'Do what?' Larry looked puzzled.

'Goodnight him. Something I've learned from Uncle Charlie Goodnight. He always put bulls in his early trail-drives and found he was losing a lot of them. They got bruised up and swelled like this one's. Head back for the house and get me some grassrope, real thin, Larry.'

Larry swung his horse. He did not hesitate as he sent his horse leaping forward headed back for the ranch. He made a fast ride, collected the thin grass rope from the store and headed back. He found that Red and Doc had thrown the bull, hogtied its forelegs and were waiting for his return. Doc held a sharp knife in his hand. He took the grassrope, stripped off a strand or two then nodded to Red. Bending, the young man forced the bull's seeds up into the skin of the belly then cut off the loosened bag of flesh. Red held down the bull's off hind leg and kept the near hind held up while watching Doc work. Red could have done this as well, or nearly as well as Doc, but the slim young man was better at the next and most important part. The wound left must be stitched up so it would not open again, if it did, the operation was a failure for the seeds would come down again but without the protective bag.

Doc moved fast, punching holes in the flesh and carefully winding the grassrope fibre through the holes made, then drawing the edges up together. When he finished the job he nodded to Red and let clear, swinging back on to his black

82

horse. Red released the legs of the moaning, struggling animal and leapt for his saddle. The bull came up with a bellow and Red swung afork his horse.

'What good's that done?' Larry asked. 'You castrated him.'

'Nope, just cut off the bag. Give him a week and he'll be back out there chasing the little gal cows ragged again and bellowing coarse as he ever did,' Red answered. 'We'll take him back to the spread and leave him in the corral where we can keep an eye on him.'

'You mean he'll be all right?'

'Why sure. Colonel Charlie always does it to his bulls when they start showing age. He allows it might not make a young bull out of an old'n, but it does keep an old'n going a piece longer,' Red Blaze replied. 'Lead him back, boy.'

'That's what they call Goodnighting a bull,' Doc remarked. 'I've been thinking of setting up as a doctor and do the same on old gents.'

The three young men headed back to the ranch, leading the bull with them and leaving it in one of the two corrals which were at the back of the house. Larry was dubious about the success of the operation although he had to admit the bull did not look any the worse for the Goodnighting.

A week later it was still all right, bellowing as coarse as ever and Larry admitted that the two cowhands knew what they were talking about. He was explaining this to one of the other hands, then turned as Red called him over.

'Saddle up, Larry, and you, Song. We'll head out and see how the stock herd is.'

The other two did as they were told, collecting their horses in a rush which showed how they liked to be out and about with Red Blaze. The three of them made good time across the range, headed for where the stock herd were grazing. The valley was just the same: the stream flowed along the bottom and the grass grew just as green and lush. There was only one thing wrong. The herd of cattle was gone.

Spurring their horses down the slope the three young cow-hands brought their horses to a halt and looked down. 'Not more'n two hours back,' Red snapped, indicating the sign.

'Rustlers?' Larry asked.

'Unless you think maybe the cattle just took a yen to go off by themselves, which ain't likely,' Red answered. 'Song, head back for the spread and bring the ranch crew. Tell Doc what's happened and bring them along. Wish we'd brought our rifles along with us.'

'You reckon you could hit anything with that relic of your'n?' Larry replied, for Red always boasted he was a poor shot with his old Spencer carbine.

'Nope. It's just nice to tote it along. It likes to go out for a ride now and then. Let's go.'

Song grunted. He did not like the idea of leaving when there was the chance of a fight, but he knew better than waste time arguing at a time like this. Swinging his horse he lit out for the ranch, riding as fast as the horse would run. There would be several men with the cattle and a rustler would always fight. With a rope or a long stretch in the State Penitentiary waiting for them rustlers would always fight. Red and Larry were going after the gang right now. Two men would not be enough to handle them.

Larry and Red rode side by side. They did not speak for a time. Red was concentrating on the sign, trying to estimate how many men were handling the herd. Larry was thinking of what would happen when they caught up. He wore a revolver and was a reasonable shot with it but he'd never used the Colt on a man before. He knew that he was not even as good with a gun as was Red, who insisted that he was the veriest beginner when it came to weapons. Not that Larry or the other members of the ranch crew believed him, they'd seen him use his guns and knew that he was good.

'Say Red,' Larry spoke up. 'They're headed for the Ranse from the look of the sign. That means they use Dead Horse Ford, it's the only place where they could move cattle across in a hurry and they'll be in a hurry.'

'That figgers,' Red agreed. He did not know the country as well as the other man and was going along with Larry's thinking. The rustlers would not know how long they'd be unpursued and would not want to waste any time in trying to swim the herd across a difficult stretch of water if they could find a reasonable ford.

'We can head for the ford and get after them.'

There was a problem facing them right now. The herd might be taken across the Ranse River and if it was, by taking the shortest and most direct route for the ford, they would save time. If the rustlers were not headed for the river, they would be wasting time for they were going to have to search for the tracks again. It was an even gamble, one way or the other. Red gave the matter some thought as they rode along the line. The rustlers would have to drive across S.S.C. and Lazy W land if they were not going to cross the river. They would be risking detection from any of the crew of either ranch who might be about. Most likely they were taking the herd over the river.

'All right, Larry.' Red made his decision. 'Head for the ford by the fastest way you know. If we miss out we'll have to come back this way and follow them.'

Larry turned his horse and headed across the range, going by a route which would have been impossible for men handling a herd of cattle. Red followed the other man's lead, trusting Larry's knowledge of the range. They rode at a fast trot yet held the horses in, for speed might be necessary later. Red was wishing he was afork his claybank for he was riding one of his string today and giving the stallion a well deserved rest. The horse he rode was all right, trained for cattlework, but did not have the speed of the claybank stallion.

They came to the Ranse River and rode the short distance along the banks, making for the ford. Red brought his horse to a halt and pointed down into the shallows. The body of a big bass lay on its side in the water, a real big bass, weighing perhaps ten or more pounds.

'Old Mossyhorn,' Larry remarked. 'I've seen him more than once in his hole. What's that thing in his jaws?'

Red swung down from the saddle, tossing the reins to Larry and then sliding down the bank. He stood in the ankle-deep water and picked up the dead bass by the thing which hung from its mouth. The weight of the dead fish dragged it loose and Red looked down at what appeared to be a grasshopper shape thing made or rubber and with three triangle hooks in it.

'Looks like Sunshine Sam got into the big feller after all,' Larry remarked. 'I remember he brought that thing back with him from town on the day before he was killed. Called it a phantom.'

Red took his handkerchief out and wrapped the phantom in it. 'Where'd he get it, I've never seen anything like it.'

'Nor me, didn't say. He just showed it us and told us that it was going to win him some money. Went out, him and the boys, they didn't come back again. We went out and found their bodies.'

Thrusting the phantom, wrapped in his handkerchief into his levis pocket Red climbed back up the slope and mounted his horse. 'Let's get on to that ford, we've wasted time enough now.'

Riding on again they came to the ford and Larry gave a sigh of relief. The sign was plain, the herd was driven across the stream here. The water was still muddy and the hoof sign made Red bring his horse to a halt and examine it more closely. The herd was not far in front of them and from the look of things did not cross easily. The rustlers appeared to have had trouble in taking the herd across although it should not have taken them any effort at all. The water here was not deep enough to give the cattle any concern, the sun was, if anything, behind them. No driven beef liked to enter water with the sun in its eyes so it could not see the other side. There was not even this cause of trouble here.

'Good work, Larry. You called it right. Let's go across and see where they're headed.'

They sent their horses into the muddy water, it was not even deep enough to wet their boots as they rode across. On the other side they allowed their horses to make better time for the tracks were fresh and easy to follow. Ahead they heard, faintly, but growing louder all the time, the sound of cattle moving.

Topping a rim the two men looked down on the herd, it was

below them and being hazed along by nine men, too big a bunch for so small a herd if it was being driven legitimately. The men, for all their number, seemed to be having trouble in handling the cattle. Far more trouble than experienced rustlers would have. One thing which could always be said for a rustler was that he was a tophand with cattle. He needed to be, for fast handling was of vital importance to him.

'They're not nesters riding the herd,' Larry remarked. 'But they're headed right for Wilben's place. It's just over that rim there.'

Red was watching the cattle and hardly heard what the other cowhand was saying. Then the import of the words struck him. He lifted his eyes from the herd to the rim ahead of them, on the other side of it smoke curled into the air. He saw that although the herd was down below them and headed away the men at the point were swinging it to line on the house. In that instant he saw it all.

'Let's go!' Red barked the order and swung his horse in a direct line towards the slope, not at the herd.

'Herd's down there, Red!' Larry yelled as he sent his horse after Red's. 'What're you going this way for?'

'They're going to stampede that herd over the Wilben place,' Red shouted back. 'They're not rustlers, can't handle cattle well enough for them to be.'

There was no time for more talk. The two horses were hitting the best speed they could manage. Down the slope the two men raced, sitting their horses with that ease which every cowhand showed in the saddle. They were both well mounted, Larry on his favourite, go-to-town horse, a leggy and fast bay and Red afork a powerful bay coyote which was generally conceded too fast for cattlework. They were riding these horses as what they were on amounted to a *pasear* rather than a working trip. Right now speed was of far more importance than good handling qualities. Red, a light rider, despite his size, handled his horse like the master he was, sending it at a far better pace, bounding and reaching out down the slope.

Racing his bay, Larry followed Red, riding in close in the mad race. Excitement tingled his cheeks, wild excitement like he'd never known before. The route they were taking would bring them to the rim in front of the herd, after that he was willing to follow any lead Red Blaze cared to make. Then he heard a scattered volley of shots and the steers were running in a wild stampede, the nine men hazing them and encouraging them to run faster than trying to halt them. Larry knew for certain Red was calling the play right, the men were not rustlers at all and they were trying to stampede it across the nesters' cultivated land.

Three of the wild riding men around the herd turned their horses from the line and came hurtling towards the two cowhands, guns in their hands. Larry watched them although Red did not appear to be giving them any attention at all. His eyes flickered in their direction just once, then were back on the route they were riding. It was then Larry saw the men were all masked. Real rustlers would not be, not while travelling with the herd off the ranch land from where they stole it. Masked men would attract attention and no rustler wanted to do that. Larry's gun was in his hand, but he held his fire. He saw a flame flicker from the Colt of one of the riders, but did not hear the bullet. This was not unexpected for it would have taken a lucky shot to hit at that range when riding a fast running horse. Larry lifted his own Colt but Red snapped, 'Don't waste lead yet.'

The two parties swept together, converging with each raking stride of the horses. Red's right hand twisted palm out and lifted the long-barrelled gun from leather and lined it, firing once. The nearest man gave a hoarse cry and rocked back in his saddle, then slowly crumpled sideways from the horse. Larry lined and fired twice. He saw the second of the men clutch at his shoulder and bring his horse to a one-handed halt, sliding it on to its rump to avoid the next shot which might be coming his way. The last man brought his horse to a halt also, swinging down from the saddle and tossing the reins over the horse's head, then pulling the rifle from the saddle-boot.

'Yeeah!' Red's wild rebel yell shattered the air. His horse left the ground in a bound and lit down making better speed, while Larry's bay flung itself out in a desperate attempt to keep up. 'Flatten down over the horn, Larry!' Red followed his yell with this warning. 'Rifle!'

Larry did not understand for a moment, then he heard the flat slapping sound made by a close-passing bullet. He fanned the horse's ears with his hat and the bay responded with a fresh burst of speed. He caught alongside Red and saw the other grinning. Red whirled the Colt on his finger, twisted it around and holstered it. 'Just like home!' he whooped. 'We're gaining on them, boy.'

The two horses were gaining on the herd, for a whiteface could not make the sort of speed a Texas longhorn could. The men urging the herd fired a few wild shots after the fast-riding cowhands but the range was too great. It was also getting too great for the man with the rifle for he was not shooting. He'd taken Larry's hat off with one shot but that was the nearest he'd come to making a hit.

Topping the rim Red and Larry saw Wilben and his two oldest sons standing staring up at them. The nester and his boys were working at cutting hay and lines of it were ready for collecting in the wagon which stood without a team but nearly full, on a level piece of ground halfway down the slope.

There was no time for much at all. Red gave a yell of 'Stampede, get to your house!'

Wilben might be plump but he was neither slow moving, nor slow thinking. He knew what that ominous rumbling was well enough and only needed the yelled warning to galvanise him into action. He snapped out an order and his sons started down the slope at a run with him following.

Red and Larry came down the slope and swung from their horses. Red bent and laid a hand on the hay. 'Bone dry, Larry. Lay a pile of it along here and watch for the herd.'

Larry grabbed up a pitchfork and with Red working by his side made a long wall of hay. Wilben saw what was happening and guessed what Red was thinking of. He turned and came back, his oldest son, the one who'd been with him in town and who'd attracted Waco's attention, followed him. They grabbed up their pitchforks and went to work. The lead steers of the herd came into sight over the rim top and Red barked, 'Run for it all of you.'

There was no arguing now. The men started down the slope at a run. Larry suddenly realised Red was not with him. Then Sandy Wilben spun around, clutching his shoulder and stumbling. Larry grabbed the young nester by the arm, got him across his shoulders and went off as fast as he could.

Reaching into his pocket, Red took out a match and rasped it on his pants. He bent and applied the tiny tongue of flame to the hay, watching the fire leap from strand to strand. He ignored the shots which were now being thrown at him as the wind caught the flames, fanning them along the line of hay. He saw the half-crazed cattle boiling down the slope towards the leaping flames, still being hazed on by the masked men. He knew that nothing but fire would stop stampeding cattle and it needed to be a fair-sized fire at that. He did not know if the small fire would do the trick. There was no time to do anything more right now except hope. He turned and saw Wilben; Larry and the other boy were almost at the house.

The bay coyote horse was standing with reins hanging as it was trained to do but its ears were flattened back and it fiddle-footed as it felt the intense heat of the fire. He ran back to the horse, caught the saddlehorn and vaulted afork, catching up the reins and setting his Kelly petmakers to work. The horse left the ground and headed down the slope. He was halfway down the slope when the horse took lead and started to go down. Red kicked his feet free of the stirrup irons and landed running even as the horse hit the ground. He felt the wind of other shots as he raced down the slope, covering the ground with raking strides in spite of his high-heeled cowhand boots. The others were all in the house by now, Wilben holding the door open. Red dived the last few feet, right through the door and with perfect timing Wilben slammed the heavy wood closed. He heard the thuds as bullets struck the door but they could not pierce the thick timber. Then he turned and watched Red Blaze getting to his feet.

It took a lot to put Red off his stride and he grinned cheerily at Wilben's plump, happy wife and his two daughters. The woman's face was not cheerful now as she worked on her son's shoulder.

'What happened?' Wilben asked as Red went to the window.

'It turned them,' Red replied. 'I was scared they might not turn at the fire.'

'What happened? How did the stampede start?'

'It was our stock herd. Run off. Larry and me trailed the men who did it. They came this way.'

'Rustlers?'

'Nope, they took it to stampede it over your place.'

'How do you figure that out?' Wilben studied the young man now.

'Easy, they drove it right at your place. Had they been rustlers they'd have stayed clear of anywhere they could be seen.'

Wilben was not looking from the window and watching the remnants of the herd scattering away. 'Why would they do a thing like that?'

'To start up trouble between the cowhands and you. The same sort of way they tried when they raided the S.S.C. and killed young Silver.'

Sandy Wilben looked up. His face was scared and worried again. He opened his mouth, then closed it again and sat still as his mother did what she could with his wound.

The masked men were coming down the slope now, most of them holding rifles. They started to take up cover behind stumps, rocks and one landed behind the dead horse. Wilben watched this and said, 'Looks like they want a fight.'

'All right, we'll make a try at giving them one,' Red replied.

CHAPTER NINE

THE FIGHT AT WILBEN'S

THE Wilben house was built on the same lines as most other such places. The front of the house was one big room which served as dining and sitting-room. Behind this was a passage and on the other side of this, kitchen and bedrooms. Red did not need to be shown the rest of the house. One could guess what it was like. In his run down the slope he'd seen enough to know that only from the front, on the slope could any serious attack develop. The land at the back and the sides was too open and did not offer any cover for the attacking men.

The next thing to occupy Red's attention was the state of defence the place was in. He saw they were not as well off as they might be. Wilben was holding a Henry rifle and his wife laid a box of .44 rimfire bullets out for him. This appeared to be his only weapon, apart from a long, old but beautifully chased, Kentucky rifle which hung on pegs over the fire. A powder horn scraped so thin that the level of the powder could be seen through the sides, and with a measure fitted to the top; and a bullet bag, hung over the gun. Red gave the old muzzle-loading gun little attention; he was thinking of cartridge weapons. He and Larry only carried their revolvers with them. Red cursed the inspiration which made him leave his old Spencer carbine behind. He was a good enough shot with either hand to make his Colts dangerous to the men if they came into anything like pistol range. They were armed with rifles and knowing the kind of men they were Red did not think they would take a single chance unless they were forced to do so.

A bullet slapped into the wall and Red flattened himself to

look out of the window. The gunmen were settling down with their rifles at about sixty yards which was beyond anything like the range of their Colt guns. It was also beyond the range at which the old Henry would be anything like accurate. The Henry was a fairly reliable repeating weapon and in its day was the best money could buy. However, even its most ardent supporters could not claim it was accurate over any range. The combination of the flat-nosed, two hundred and sixteen grain bullet and the weak, twenty-six grain powder charge made accuracy at ranges of over fifty yards uncertain to say the least.

The men on the slope were not much better off for most of them appeared to be armed with Winchester Model 73's. These were a better all-round rifle than their grandfather, the Henry, but still did not have enough power to drive a ball through the thick log walls of the house.

'Get your lady into the back of the house. Send your boy. He's hurt and can't help us any,' Red said to Wilben, watching the slope all the time.

A man slid in behind a rock and Red knew straight off he was going to make trouble. That man was holding a Sharps Old Reliable rifle. The Sharps might be a singleshot weapon but it could be reloaded fast enough by a man who knew what he was doing. It would hold true at half a mile or more and would retain enough power to knock down a full grown buffalo bull at the end. The rifle roared and smoke rolled from behind the rock; the heavy .50 bullet came through the wall like it was tarpaper and gouged a splinter-throwing groove in the top of the oak table top.

'Quick, ma'am!' Red checked the woman's objection to leaving her husband. 'He'll shoot this place plumb full of holes and with all of us here he'll connect with some of it. The less here the less chance he has of doing any harm.'

'Do as the young man says, Martha,' Wilben said mildly. 'He's acting for the best.'

Another bullet from the Sharps hit the wall and burst clear through, kicking up splinters near Sandy Wilben's feet. The young man was pale from the shock of his wound and from something more which was worrying him. His mother came forward and helped him leave the room, then ushered the rest of the family out after. She came back to lay a hand on Larry's shoulder. 'That was a brave thing you did out there young man. Thank you for saving my son.'

Larry blushed. He smiled at the woman. 'Shucks, ma'am. I only did what he'd done for me. You best get out of here, ma'am.'

The window frame smashed as a bullet from the Sharps struck it, sending glass flying. Red ducked back instinctively, then growled, 'We got to get that Sharps gun and get him fast.'

Larry took Mrs. Wilben, led her to the door of the room and opened it. He gave her a reassuring smile and said, 'Don't you go fretting, we'll get you out of this and we'll take care of your man for you. Ole Red there rode as a Lieutenant in the Texas Light Cavalry. He can handle any bunch like them.'

Closing the door on the woman Larry took his place by the other window and looked out. He took time to reload the empty chamber of his Colt and push a bullet into the usually empty sixth chamber. This was a safety precaution, for no man liked to carry a revolver loaded with six bullets when riding a horse. Red watched him with approval, Larry was growing up fast. He'd make a good foreman for the spread if Waco did not stay on at the end of the trouble.

Once more the Sharps rifle boomed and a hole appeared in the wall. Wilben gave a startled curse and ducked back, holding his face.

'They get you?' Red asked.

'Splinters is all. We've got to stop him, Red.'

'Mister, you've never been more right than now.' Red turned and looked at the Kentucky rifle again. 'The old gun work?'

'Sure. Sandy bought it when we came out here. He's kept it clean and uses it to bark squirrels with.'

'Mind if I use it?' Red darted across the room and lifted rifle, powder flask and bullet bag down. He hefted the bag and was relieved to find it was full of ready-moulded balls. Returning to the window he knelt down. 'This old gun's got the range over that Henry.'

'What do you want me to do?' Wilben was willing to let Red run the fight.

'Keep their heads down. Don't let them get in too close. Larry, you let a few shots off, not too many, we've only got the loads in our bullet loops to fall back on.'

Leaving the other two men to get on with their tasks Red started to load the old gun, working with a speed which showed he knew what he was doing. First he poured a measure of powder into the barrel from the flask. Opening the patch-box he took out a well-greased felt patch from the pile of them which filled the box. He put the patch in the muzzle of the rifle, took the roundest ball he could find, placed this on the patch and rammed both home. There was neither flurry nor nervousness in the way he acted. He primed the frizzen pan, checked the flint was held firmly. He hefted the rifle with appreciation, knowing it to be as fine an example of the gun-maker's art as was ever made. He'd handled these fine, long, old rifles before and knew their secrets.

'How's she fire?' he asked.

'About three inch high and just a mite to the left at seventy-five yards.' Wilben could see that here was a man who knew well how to shoot, a man who could handle the old Kentucky even better than he himself could.

Red brought the rifle up, lining through the window. He felt the smooth curve of the butt nestle into his shoulder and the balance the forty-inch barrel gave. He focused the V notch of the backsight and pinhead sight at the tip of the barrel. His aim was not at the man but the small rock in front of where the Sharps user was hidden. The old rifle cracked. For an instant smoke obscured Red's vision but it quickly dispersed and he saw a dark blotch on the rock right where it should be if Wilben called the sights right. Red was ready to take the Sharps user right now. Even as he primed and reloaded the Kentucky he marvelled at the way it held its accuracy. The gun held as true as the day, which was not just a couple of years back, when some gunsmith along the banks of the Ohio

95

River made it in his small shop. It was still accurate enough to bring off the honoured, old time trick of barking a squirrel. Barking squirrels was a trick attributed to Daniel Boone and required a steady aim, also an accurate rifle. It came about in the old days. A man could only take one weapon along with him, mostly only possessed one, when he went hunting, bad whites and hostile Indians, a man took along his .45 calibre Kentucky rifle when he went out. A squirrel was a delicacy but when shot with a rifle like the Kentucky was messy. A man did not need to skin it out, the bullet spread the squirrel. So barking was discovered. To do it a man aimed, not at the squirrel but at the branch just under the animal. If the shot was made correctly the bark splinters flying up, killed it as well and more cleanly than a direct hit.

Waiting his chance Red lined the rifle. The man with the Sharps was getting over-confident through the lask of opposition to his long shooting rifle. He sent another bullet through the wall and watched the other members of his bunch moving closer in, soon they would be at a range where their Winchesters could also throw lead through the walls. He came up more leisurely and lined his gun carefully. One of the logs of the cabin looked as if it might be splitting and a couple more shots would speed the process.

Bringing the Kentucky up Red lined and fired, holding as steady as a rock even though bullets were coming through the window. The heavy boom of the Sharps was answered by the flatter bark of the Kentucky. The old muzzle loader kicked up and smoke hid Red's man from him but, with the instinct of a good shot, Red knew he'd made a meat-pie-in-the-pot hit.

'Yowee!' Larry hooped. 'You got him, Red!'

'Clean through the chest, friend,' Wilben went on, just as enthusiastic at the shooting.

Red looked through the window and could see no sign of the man, although the Sharps rifle lay on this side of the rock. The gunmen on the slope certainly aimed to try and get the Sharps back. While the others poured lead down the slope and at the house, three darted for the rock. Wilben's Henry beat a tattoo as fast as he could work the lever and fire it. One of the running men stopped in his tracks, then crumpled down, rolling over. The other two hurled themselves the last few feet and were behind the rock.

The barrel of a Winchester came into view around the side of the rock, trying to hook the Sharps and drag it in. Red tipped the bullet-pouch and spilled the balls into his hand. He examined them carefully and picked the most perfect. There was only going to be time for one shot and it needed to be accurate. That Sharps must not be allowed to fall into the hands of the gunmen again. Realising the value of the Sharps to their plans the men up the slope fired fast, sending their bullets through the windows in an attempt to hold the defenders down. It prevented any chance of the Kentucky being rested on the windowsill and for a shot like this a steadier rest than human arms was required.

Fast action was needed for the man was drawing the rifle slowly to a position where it could be grabbed by a quick, snatching arm. Red did not hesitate for a moment. 'Larry, come over here and kneel down.'

Larry obeyed fast. He also knew the urgency of the situation and moved back into the room, kneeling in front of Red and allowing the barrel of the Kentucky to rest on his shoulder Red bent and lined the rifle, aiming up the slope to where he could see the rifle sliding along slowly, inching to where the men waited for it. The room reverberated to the crack of Wilben's Henry as he recklessly exposed himself, trying to draw the fire from Red's window and allow the Texan an uninterruped shot at the Sharps.

Calmly Red issued orders, his voice steadying Larry. 'Down a mite, little more. Up a touch, now down. Hold it there!'

The sights lined, moving along the barrel of the Sharps, towards the breech, knowing this was the only place where a hit might permanently damage the rifle. Allowing for the slight cavagry of the sights Red squeezed the trigger. The sear released, the hammer fell, propelling flint down, kicking a spark into a frizzen and the priming powder. There was a faint hiss as the powder fired and ignited the charge in the barrel and sent the bullet winding up, patch catching in the rifling and turning it. The Kentucky rifle cracked and even through the smoke Red saw the Sharps kick but whether from his shot or the pull of the other rifle he could not tell. The men behind the rock must have guessed what was wrong for one shot out an arm and grabbed the Sharps, pulling it in.

Larry straightened up, grinning broadly. Old Red was a ringtailed ripper with a rifle and that was for sure. He might try and say he was no sort of shot but when the chips were down he showed he could call his shots with skill.

Up on the slope, hidden behind a stump, a voice called, 'You got that Sharps, Hal?'

'Sure, but they hit the breech and bust it to hell. Jack is dead!'

The big man kneeling behind the rock made a wry face behind his mask, not at the death of the gunman, but at the loss of the rifle. His original nine men were reduced to six and one of them wounded. If they were going to get that bunch in the house they were going to need some real fast thinking and action. His five friends were good fighting men but those two cowhands were also good, especially that damned red-haired Tejano. Fighting from the cover of the house he would do plenty of damage before they got at him.

A man darted forward joining the one who'd called out for information about the gun. 'They got Jack, Cholla.' Not even the mask could hide the rage this man was showing.

'Sure Ted, they got Jack.' Cholla Jocelyn was not as interested in the death of the Sharps user as the big man. After all, Jack Kell was the man's brother and as close as only a hardcase Kentucky hill farmer could get. 'We have got to get them out of there and real fast. Those two from the S.S.C. might be missed and the rest of the crew will be coming out to look for them.'

Ted Kell was not worrying over that. His brother was dead and he would never rest until the men who did it also lay dead. 'We're going to get them out, all right.'

There was hatred in the man's snarl, yet there was also a fight-wise caution in him which would not allow anything foolish. Kell was born and raised in the feud country of the Kentucky hills. He knew hate of an enemy must be controlled. Any wild charging attack on that house would end in disaster from the very start. The men inside were all able to handle their weapons. There was another and easier way of doing this. Kell's eyes went to the hay-wagon.

'I'll start the boys moving in again.'

Kell turned as Cholla Jocelyn spoke. 'Ain't no need to risk us losing men. That hay wagon'll roll right down there and smash into the house front. All we need to do is light a match, put it to the hay and let her go. It'll burn them clear out.'

Jocelyn grinned. He was wondering why he hadn't thought of this himself. The hay was dry and would flare up just as well as when that red-headed cowhand used it to stop the stampeding cattle. It would be even worse, for the great pile would flare up just as readily and the wind would fan it higher as the wagon raced down the slope. It would be a roaring, unquenchable mass by the time it smashed into the front of the tinder dry house. There would be no holding the fire then for the house would go up, becoming a funeral pyre for the defenders.

'Get the boys here!' Jocelyn snapped. 'It'll take all of us to turn that wagon and get it started.'

In the house Red watched the slope with the other men. He saw the gunmen making for the hay-wagon. Larry turned towards him and grinned. 'Looks like General Meade exhorting his veterans.'

Red did not smile, he snapped, 'You got a cellar to the house?'

'Sure, a small one. Trapdoor's in here, under the table.'

'Get your wife and family down it then, and go yourself.'

Wilben wondered at the note of urgency in Red's voice. Since the Sharps rifle stopped barking he'd felt that the worst was over; that the men on the slope would spend some more time in long distance shooting then pull out. He was not even wasting any more ammunition on the men as they gathered behind the—

'Lord. You think they'd——?'

'I don't *think*, mister. I *know*. Move!'

Wilben moved fast. He'd heard that note in a voice before. It was the voice of a martinet officer. Pulling open the door he went through and out of sight. Red wasted no time; he jerked a hand towards the table and told Larry to move the table then lift the trapdoor ready.

'What're we going to do, Red?'

'*You're* going down the cellar.'

Larry caught the emphasis on the first word and got just what Red meant. 'Like hell I am. You're not sending me down there with those folks while you go outside and—— What the hell do you think I am, Red?'

Red grinned at the other young man. 'A damned fool. All right, you stay on up here.'

Wilben came in followed by his family. The woman stopped and looked at Red who was checking the loads of his revolvers and Larry who stood by the door.

'What're you going to do?' she asked.

'Nothing, ma'am. You go down there and stay down. Take *all* your family with you.'

Sandy Wilben stood with his arm in a sling. He darted to the window and looked up the slope. The gunmen were trying to turn the wagon and he knew what they were doing it for. He also realised what Red meant to do. 'I'm not going down there when that bunch are planning to——'

Red did not argue, or hesitate, his right fist came round to crash into Sandy's jaw. Larry caught the young nester and pulled him across the floor. 'Sorry, ma'am. He fainted. Get him down there.'

Red swung back to the window again. He did not know what the Wilben family thought of his actions in knocking Sandy out but he was not even going to waste time finding out. The gunmen up the slope were swinging the hay-wagon slowly around. It was hard work for men on foot and none of them thought of getting their horses. Red looked at the old Kentucky rifle and wondered if he could get one or two of the men with it. The range was even greater than when he'd used it on the Sharps user, at least a hundred yards, and that was a long shot for a Kentucky. There would not be time to load the old rifle fast enough to do any good with it.

Wilben licked his lips. He'd seen his family safe down into

100

the cellar and came across the room, picking up the Henry rifle and levering a bullet into the chamber. 'Get down the cellar, friend,' Red said gently.

'No. I'm going out there with you.'

Up on the slope the gunmen strained and heaved on the wagon as they swung it around to point down the slope. Cholla Jocelyn snarled out a curse as a thought struck him. 'Hold it!'

The straining men relaxed and waited to hear what was worrying Jocelyn. Kell snarled out, a match in his hand. 'What's wrong now, Cholla?'

'Get the hosses here. If any of them get out they'll be coming through that door at the back. We want to get around there ready for them and we can't do it on foot. Besides there'll be some smoke and folks'll be coming on the run. We've got to load Jack and Frank on their hosses ready to take them with us. You know the boss don't want any bodies leaving behind.'

Three of the men darted off to get the horses and returned fast, riding down the slope and slinging the two bodies across the saddles of two riderless mounts. Then they returned to the wagon and Kell growled impatiently at the delay. He was like a savage, his eyes flaring as he reached for the match again and rasped it on his pants, then set the hay alight, watching the flames leap and spread. Then he moved back to his horse and jerked the rifle from the saddleboot. He knew the men in the house could see what was going on. He also knew they would not tamely stand by and let it happen. They would be coming out of the building and up the slope in an attempt to get within range so they could use their handguns. He was going to make sure they did not get the chance to do it. Without a word to the others he slipped down the slope and flopped down behind a rock, his Spencer rifle cuddled into his shoulder and lifted the sights.

Red Blaze hefted his right-hand gun. He saw Larry's face was just a trifle pale but the young man looked steady enough. 'Let's go!' Red said, 'You open the door, mister.'

Wilben did it without suspecting a thing. Red jerked his head to the cellar and Larry went to lift the trapdoor again.

Then Red's pistol lifted to land on Wilben's head and knock him down. The man was dazed and before he could recover Red was pulling him to the trapdoor. Larry helped lower Wilben down then heard Red say, 'Never trust anybody, boy.'

Red's shoulder came round and thrust Larry into the cellar after Wilben, his foot kicked down the door and he ran across the room. Opening the house door Red drew a breath. Jerking the door open he leapt out, running for the foot of the slope.

Kell's breath let out a savage snarl as his eyes lined the sights of his rifle on the weaving, fast-running man while above him the other gunmen inched the wagon towards the edge of the incline.

CHAPTER TEN

MOLLY BREAKS HER ENGAGEMENT

MOLLY WILMONT was bored. The wailing screech of the string quartet got on her nerves. The thin-faced leader annoyed her by the way he screwed up his face in what he fondly imagined was a look of rapture but which resembled someone who'd been sucking on a lump of alum. She stood by the double doors of the sitting-room of the Wellington house and tried to look as if she were enjoying herself. Glancing sideways at the mirror on the wall she half approved, half hated, what she saw: a tall, slim, black-haired and beautiful young woman dressed to the height of fashion. The frock, leaving her shoulders bare, was tight and constraining to someone who'd been used to more casual clothes. Her face was losing its tan now and taking on the socially acceptable pallor which she so disliked.

Across the room Laverne and Alvine Wellington were tittering and whispering behind their fans. She watched them and felt disgusted. They were something she hated, simpering flirts who lived for two things only, gossip and flirtations. They and the others of their kind in the room did not interest her; they'd nothing in common. By the punchbowl Mrs. Wellington stood erect, her thin, pointed face showing disapproval at something or other. Molly did not like Mrs. Wellington any more than her two daughters, nor did Mrs. Wellington particularly like her.

Looking around the room Molly hoped that her fiancé, Keith Wellington, had arrived. There was no sign of him, or his father, the bluff, hearty Sam, a man she could like and admire. The old man was rich now, very rich, but he'd earned his money the hard way though he was reputed to be one of the richest men in Chicago. Money would not change him but his wife had done so. Mrs. Wellington was an arrant snob, a sourfaced arbiter of what she thought was good taste.

The piece of music ended to polite applause and Molly wished she could find an excuse to leave. There was no hope of that. Mrs. Wellington's plans for the day included this musical afternoon, then a visit to a theatre. There was no avoiding either. She must sit through the agony of the music all afternoon, then attend the dry as dust play that evening. She wished Keith were here. Keith was some boy and she loved him but she wished he would relax more. He'd taken her around with him to the usual social round, visits to the Streeterville Sporting Club where the bloods of upper-class Chicago foregathered. He'd taken her riding and proved to be good on a horse, though not as good as the youngest cowhand working on the Lazy W, but that was to be expected. Molly, knew that riding for a living was different to riding for sport. He'd taken her to a meeting of the Streeterville Rifle Club and displayed skill with a rifle although she was amused at the way he and his friends handled revolvers. They could shoot good groups on a target at twenty-five yards but she'd seen men who could do better. For all of that she loved Keith and knew that, given a chance, and away from his mother, he would be all man.

'Miss Wilmont.' Molly turned at the disapproving voice of Limbkin the butler. 'There are two persons asking for you at the front door.'

'Who are they?' Molly knew Limbkin did not approve of her and she didn't like him.

'I did not inquire. They are not the sort of people madam would encourage to come visiting.'

'What is it, Molly dear?' Mrs. Wellington was by Molly's elbow, frowning. 'Monsieur le Beaufort is just going to per-form again.'

'Somebody's asking for me at the door,' Molly answered, seeing the leader of the quartet lifting his bow.

'Dear me. I do hope they are not like the last ones.'

Molly bit down an angry retort. Early in her acquaintance with the Wellington family a cowhand and his wife came to visit her while on a trip to Chicago. Mrs. Wellington arrived in time to hear Molly entertaining her guests, Mr. and Keith Wellington and a prominent railway president to a rowdy and slightly bawdy cowhand song. There'd been some unpleasant scenes over that and Mrs. Wellington never gave Molly a chance to forget it. It was only because of Sam Wellington's intervention that the engagement did not end then. He swore that he'd never heard the song done better.

Turning on her heel Molly went towards the door. She could not think who would be visiting her here. There were few enough people in Chicago who knew her, outside the circle of the Wellington family. Whoever they were they did not meet with Limbkin's approval. Then, nobody apart from Mrs. Wellington did. She opened the doors before Limbkin could arrive and forestall her. It always annoyed him. She went to the front door and a liveried footman drew it open for her. She didn't know what to expect and stared, hardly believing her eyes. She gave a most unladylike whoop. 'Rusty!'

'Hi Molly.' Mary Anne stepped forward and the two girls hugged each other.

'Say what're you doing here?' Molly asked, her pleasure at seeing her old friend making her forget where she was. Behind her the doors were open and the music came to a stop as everyone turned to see what the noise was about.

'Came to see you, gal.' Mary Anne grinned delightedly. 'Say, you remember my lil brother, Waco.'

Before Molly could answer there was an interruption. Mrs. Wellington was standing there, a vinegar sour scowl on her face. 'Molly!'

'I'd like you to meet——' Molly began.

Mrs. Wellington ignored the girl, looking Mary Anne and Waco up and down. They were still wearing the clothes they'd bought at the Texas railhead and these were not to the best of fashion. She sniffed then said, 'Tell your friends to go round the back to the kitchen if they want a meal. And I would like to see you immediately in the library.'

Molly's face turned red, wild anger in her eyes. She swung to Mary Anne. 'You come in a Victoria?'

'Sure,' Mary Anne was annoyed. She knew she was not well dressed, but there was no call for such impoliteness.

'Wait for me in it. This won't take long.'

Mary Anne and Waco watched the girl following the sour-faced woman into a side room. The annoyance at once left Mary Anne. She turned and grinned at Waco. 'Man, there'll be some fur flying soon. I haven't seen ole Molly so wild since she caught Susan Mae O'Dea with the boy who'd brought her to the quilting party. Come on.'

Molly went into the library with fire in her eyes. Mrs. Wellington was waiting for her and the Wellington girls, tittering behind their fans, were also in the room. Mrs. Wellington looked at Molly with the scowl she usually saved for her social inferiors.

'I have asked you repeatedly not to associate with those low people, Molly. After all, when you are married to a Wellington you——'

The door opened and Keith Wellington came in. He was a tall, fair, handsome and well built young man, his well-cut suit emphasizing his powerful figure. He came forward, face worried for he'd seen that look on his mother's face before and knew what it meant. 'What's wrong, Molly?'

Molly ignored him. Her temper was up now and when that happened she was wild as a longhorned Texas steer. '*If* I marry a Wellington the first thing I'll do is get him as far away from you as I can. That girl out there is my best friend. She's more like a sister to me. She happens to own a ranch as big, if not bigger, than the Lazy W. Not that that bothers me. She could still come to visit me even if she was as poor as a Texas sharecropper and she'd be welcome. Friendship doesn't mean how much money a person has in the bank. Not to me. She was my friend and came to see me, not to be insulted.'

Laverne Wellington gave a shriek and her mother sat rigid at the girl's effrontery. Then her voice lashed out in the tone which cowed unruly business people and servants. 'Listen to me, young woman. I've never been in favour of you marrying my son. You are not the kind of person a Wellington should marry.'

'Is that right?' Molly's eyes flickered to Keith. 'What do you say to that, Keith boy?'

Keith's mouth opened and then closed. He was in an awkward spot now, torn between loyalty to his mother and love for this fiery Texas girl. He tried to smooth things over. 'Look, Molly——'

'No, you look. I'm not good enough for your family, it looks like. All right, that suits me. I didn't intend marrying all your family. If I marry you it looks as if I'd have to marry the family.' She pulled the engagement ring from her finger and threw it on to the table top. 'There, give it to some tittering, simpering flirt like these two. There's a whole lot of them out there who'd just be ready to let your mother wipe her feet on them to become a Wellington. Give that ring to one of them. You don't want a woman.'

'Don't you dare speak to my brother like that?' Laverne shouted, determined to show this girl her dislike. 'I'll——'

The words ended abruptly as Molly gripped the front of Laverne's dress and pulled the girl forward, holding a folded, hard-looking fist under her nose. 'You'll do nothing. You dumb little sheep, you couldn't walk the width of the room without a guide. It's a pity you didn't see the man who was with my friend. He'd really have set you going after some of the things I've seen you flirting with.'

Molly gave Laverne a contemptuous push which staggered her back across the room. Mrs. Wellington gave a cry and flopped back in her chair with arms hanging limp and mouth open. Molly looked at Keith. 'I'm going back to Texas. Goodbye.'

Keith was about to speak but the Wellington girls were by their mother and shrieking that she was having one of her turns. Once more he was caught in that mess. It was either the girl he loved or his mother. He'd seen enough of her turns to know how dangerous they were. Yet for all that he could not just walk away and leave her, it might be serious. Also sense told him that in her present mood Molly would not listen to any reason. Turning, Keith bent over his mother, hearing the door of the room slam behind Molly. He thought there was a flickering smile of triumph across his mother's lips.

Stamping down the passage towards the door Molly ignored the sea of faces which watched her. She knew everyone here was interested in what was going on. It would give them something to talk about for days she guessed. Limbkin was opening the door for her, a supercilious sneer on his face. There was a look of delight about him that annoyed her as he said, 'The persons are waiting in the Victoria, Miss Wilmont.'

'Why thank you most to death, Limbkin.' Molly's voice dripped with poison loaded honey. 'You remind me of a pet packrat I once had, only he was better looking, smelling and tempered. Don't drink too much of Mr. Wellington's best whisky. He'll catch you one of these days.'

With this she swept proudly through the front door, for all her poise giving the footman a broad wink and seeing an eyelid droop in the impassive face. Limbkin watched her go, frowing, shocked out of his usual blank expression by the fact that his secret incursions into Wellington's best bonded whisky were noted. He was pleased the girl was going but knew she'd left him the loser.

Mrs. Wellington was recovering when the door of the library burst open. Sam Wellington came in, his usually red face redder as he pulled open his collar and slammed the door with a bang which jarred the pictures on the wall.

'What the hell's going on?' he roared.

Laverne sniffed. 'That horrible girl said nasty things to Mama. I thought she would strike me.'

'It's a pity she didn't. Might have knocked some sense into you,' Wellington growled, then looked at his wife. 'Stop your fooling, Clara, them turns of yours don't fool me. You never had them when we lived in the badlands, down Clancy Street.'

Mrs. Wellington sat up again, her turn ending even quicker than it began. Her husband, like the few others so privileged, usually called her Clarissa, rather than by her given name of Clara. She also knew that her husband was usually mild and compliant but when he took that tone it was time to step carefully.

'Samuel——'

'Where's she now?' Wellington growled, ignoring his wife's words.

'She's left.' Keith stood looking at the ring on the table.

'So you finally did it, did you?' Wellington roared at his wife. 'You finally drove off that little girl. Before I made my pile you'd have been proud to have a gal like Molly marry our boy. You're getting so high toned and snooty you've forgot how we started out.' He turned his attention and anger on his son. 'And you. For once in your life you pick a decent gal, the sort who'll make you a good wife and make a man out of you. So what do you do, you let her get away. I'd have hoped you would show more damned sense than lose her and by hell you're not going to lose her. You're going out of this house and you don't come back until you bring her with a wedding ring on her finger. Understand?'

Keith drew himself erect. 'I understand.'

'All right, get going.'

Walking from the library Keith was aware that all eyes were on him. He turned and went to his room. Inside he began to pack his bag with a change of clothes. He knew Molly and knew that the only way to get her back was to go to Texas and win her. He knew little of the West, except what he'd read in the blood and thunder stories of Ned Buntline and what Molly told him. He could ride and hoped to get work as a cowhand until he could win her back. The door of his room opened as he packed his small bag with a change of under-clothes, that was all he would be taking with him. He did not turn around or even look up as his father's voice came to him.

'You going all the way after her, boy?'

'It's the only way.'

Sam Wellington took out his wallet, extracted a sheaf of money, dropping it by his son's hand. 'You'll likely need some of this, then. Good luck.'

Leaving his son's room Wellington went downstairs. He glared at the crowd in the room. Every eye was on him, every one giving him their attention. He'd never realised how much he disliked most of his wife's circle of friends before. The time was on hand for a revolution and Sam Wellington was the man to make it.

'Limbkin,' Wellington yelled. 'Send down to Pat O'Leary's shebeen down on Clancy Street and get a couple of bottles of his whisky.' Then turning to the pained-looking quartet leader he went on. 'Say, Horace, do you know Finnigan's Wake?'

Keith Wellington packed his bag and left, making for the Texas and Chicago Depot. He made a reservation on the night westbound train, left his grip and went to the Reed-Astoria. Entering the hall he went to the desk. 'Hello, Jules. Is Miss Wilmont in?'

'No sir. She returned and left with Mr. and Miss Catlan.'

'When will she be back?'

Jules sniffed. 'She didn't say, sir.'

Keith got it. Jules was under orders not to give anything away. He must have seen the missing engagement ring and drawn his own conclusions. Jules was a smart gent, besides, knowing Molly she'd probably given orders for her whereabouts not to be mentioned. Turning on his heel Keith left the hotel and went to the Streeterville Sporting Club to spend a miserable afternoon.

Molly was also spending a miserable afternoon. Her temper was still at boiling point when she got to the hotel. Mary Anne knew there was nothing they could do but wait for the storm to blow over. She worked on the principle that the best way to cool a woman's temper was to get her to spend some money.

'Damn all men!' Molly slung her bag on the bed. 'There's not a good one any place, they're all the same.'

'Sure are,' Marry Anne agreed, winking at Waco who was standing back and keeping quiet, showing wisdom. 'Ain't none of them worth the keeping. Let's go shopping.'

'I'm going home tonight.'

'Thought you was selling the Lazy W,' Mary Anne asnswered.

'You thought what?'

Mary Anne held out the letter and Molly took it. She read

110

the letter and her face got even more red. 'What the hell?' Molly's voice was hard. 'I never wrote this.'

'I never thought you did. Look at the spelling, it's too good for you,' Mary Anne answered. 'But it got to Colonel O'Dea.'

'Got to Colnel O'Dea.'

'Got to Colonel O'Dea?' Molly felt stupid repeating the words but her mind was not working properly.

'Sure, got to him. Look, you're not thinking properly yet. Let's go shopping and I'll explain it all to you.'

Molly agreed to this but she just could not get up enough energy yet. She looked at the letter again and shook her head. Waco came forward and Mary Anne jerked a hand to him. 'Didn't get time to introduce you to my lil brother before. This here's Waco.'

Molly grinned, holding out her hand. 'Hi, boy. Some lil brother. You growed up, boy.'

'So'd you. Who'd you write to down in Texas, Molly?'

'Colonel O'Dea, his gals. I wrote to White, a couple of the other gals, telling them about getting engaged.'

'Short letters?' Waco went on.

Mary Anne laughed. 'Short letters. She wouldn't know how.'

Molly eyed her friend. 'Listen Fatty——'

'Fatty is it?' Mary Anne answered. 'Why you——'

'Simmer down, both of you.' Waco pushed Mary Anne on to the bed and Molly into a chair. 'This's more serious than having a hair yanking. Didn't you meet anybody from Texas in the past month or so?'

'Nope, nor was I likely to. Mrs. Wellington thinks all Texans, including me, are uncouth savages, just one stage further advanced than the Indians. Mind,' Molly eyed Mary Anne and Waco, 'I'm not saying she was far wrong where some of us are concerned.'

'Sure, you Lazy W bunch were always the same, wild, woolly, full of fleas and never seen a currying below the knees. Come on, let's go shopping and make reservations on the night train. I never thought you would sell the Lazy W.' Mary Anne grinned at her friend. 'You aren't smart but you're too smart for that.'

'Yeah,' Molly snorted. 'I'm not sure with neighbours like you I'd show sense if I did sell out.' She paused and picked up her hat from where she'd thrown it. 'Why'd you pair come here anyway?'

'To show you this letter,' Waco explained. 'Lootenant Ballinger allows a Doc Pilener wrote it, Doc being found dead the day after it was posted. That means the man who did it is an Eastern man, but one that knows the Ranse River country. He wants both Lazy W and S.S.C. and with this letter he'd likely come to get them both. Colonel O'Dea would have sold him the Lazy W. and then with control of the water he could run S.S.C. off.'

'You got somebody in mind, boy?' Molly asked, watching this handsome youngster and wondering where he'd learned to act like this.

'Mebbee, mebbee not. Man never can tell and I sure don't aim to.'

Mary Anne could see that Waco did not wish to say any more on the subject and pressed that they went shopping before they pulled out of the big city. Molly took the hint and Waco was evicted while she put on a dress which, while not being so stylish was at least comfortable.

Jules studied the three as they came to the desk, noting Molly was not wearing her engagement ring now. 'If anyone comes asking for me you don't know how long I'll be gone, Jules,' Molly said grimly.

'I understand, Miss Wilmont.' In his frigid way Jules liked the Texas girl and he did not intend doing anything she would not wish him to do. 'I hope your suite is satisfactory, Miss Catlan?'

'Sure. We'll be checking out tonight.'

They'd left only a few moments when Keith arrived. That night found them all on the westbound train, headed for Texas. Molly did not even suspect Keith was on the train, nor did Keith guess the girl he loved was in a sleeper in the compartment next to his own. He sat moodily in the room for a time then rose and made his way to the smoker.

The smoker was almost deserted as he sat at one of the

tables and called for a beer. Two beefy, flashily-dressed men sat by the bar and nodded to the other. They rose, coming along to the table. 'Can we join you, friend?'

'Sure, take a seat.' Keith looked up. These men were not the sort he would have chosen to associate with in Chicago but things were done differently out west.

'Going west?' the bigger of the pair asked, offering a cigar-case.

'Texas. And you?'

'Texas, too. A fine country.' The man was heavily mous-tached, his face reddened from either sun or long exposure to the full glare of a whisky glass. He wore a loud check suit which clashed with his salmon pink shirt and big bow tie. 'I'm Joe. Sell razors, bayrum and stuff for a barbershop. This's Lou. You might not believe it but he sells ladies' corsets.'

Lou was bearded, dressed as glaringly as his friend and grinned amiably. He did not appear to be at all worried by his friend telling what he sold. 'Good things to sell. The gals are always going to wear them. Have a drink.'

The train was moving now, rattling along the rails. Keith sat back laughing at the stories the men told, stories of their adventures while travelling. They appeared to be a pair of cheery, rough diamonds and were just what he wanted now to relieve the monotony of the journey.

'Say, how about a game of poker to pass the time?' Joe asked. 'Lou here owes me a dollar fifty from our last game and I sure hate to see him win.'

Keith was just a little suspicious. He'd heard of cardsharps on trians before. His first inclination was to decline the offer but Lou shook his head. 'I don't know, Joe. We don't know this young feller. I know he looks all right but——'

Keith frowned. The man did not trust him. The feeling hurt. Here he was, a member of the Streeterville Sporting Club and this overdressed drummer did not trust him. He sat back, his mouth a tight, grim line and Joe snorted. 'You've hurt the young feller's feelings. You can't take him any place twice, they won't even have him back to apologise for the first time. I'm not playing unless our friend plays, Lou.'

Lou looked contrite. 'All right, all right. No offence, friend. It's just that there gets to be a lot of sharps on these trains. I wasn't making out that you are one. Say, to show you there's nothing in it you go get the deck of cards from the bar.'

Keith was mollified by this. He'd been doubtful but now he felt ashamed of himself. Here were two perfectly decent men and he'd thought they were crooked gamblers. Now they were going to let him get the cards showing they trusted him. He was a good poker player. The play at the Streeterville Sporting Club was often high and he'd held his own there. He might win or lose a few dollars in this game but that would not matter for his wallet was bulging and he could afford a small loss.

Taking the cards back to the table Keith sat down facing the two men. He was seated with his back to the leather seat while they were facing him across the table, yet they were well apart. Nothing could be wrong.

'What's the stakes?' Lou asked.

'Whatever you fancy.' Keith felt expansive.

'Man, we'll have to watch him, Lou,' Joe chuckled. 'He's got a gleam in his eye. Let's us set down real small and try him out. Say five cents to twenty-five.'

Keith chuckled, giving the cards a riffle. The stakes would not break him, he was going to enjoy a friendly game.

CHAPTER ELEVEN

A TOPHAND FROM CHICAGO

'HE's not there!' Molly withdrew her head from the open window.

'Isn't he?' Mary Anne sat back on the bunk of their sleeper compartment. 'Did you think he would be?'

'Me?' Molly snorted. 'I'm not in the least worried about Mr. Keith Wellington. I wouldn't speak to him if he was the last man alive.'

'Was he the last man alive I don't reckon he'd have time to worry,' Waco remarked.

'That's the sort of remark I could expect from a man.' Molly was in no mood for jollity. She'd been hoping Keith would at least come to the train and try to stop her leaving. 'Men! There's no good in any of them. The whole lot are stupid, conceited, boasting, tied to their mothers' apron strings. Where'd they be without a woman to look after them and to sew their buttons on for them?'

'If there were no women we wouldn't need the buttons.' Waco felt called on to defend the male sex in this den of womanhood.

'Very funny,' Mary Anne snorted. 'Don't worry, Molly, you'll never be troubled by him again.'

'I know.' Molly suddenly gave a sniff and flung herself on to the bunk, sobbing. 'If only he'd stood up against his mother just once.'

Waco grinned, taking up his hat and making for the door of the compartment. This was no place for a man and the sooner he got out of it the better. 'I'll go and see to my bunk,' he told Mary Anne. 'Likely see you in the diner later on.'

Waco went along two doors, opening the sleeper reserved

for him. His bag lay on the bed and the new rifle by its side. He took it up and turned it over in his hands. This was a weapon a man could be proud of, more range than a '73 and just as reliable. The Ysabel Kid would be green with envy when he saw it, might even trade in that 'One of a Thousand '73' for this kind. He cleaned the rifle and his twin Colts, then got to his feet and unbuckled the gunbelt. There did not appear to be much point in wearing it tonight. It was too far east for there to be any danger of a hold-up and a brace of matched guns weighed heavy on a man. He thrust his right-hand gun into his waistband so that his coat hid it then picked up the rifle, gunbelt and second Colt, taking them to Mary Anne's sleeper and knocking. He was let in by Molly who was over her tears now and looking annoyed at her lapse. 'Lock these away for me, Rusty gal,' he said. 'Then let's go eat.'

The meal was not a success for Molly was about as cheerful as an undertaker with a toothache. After it was over the girls were all for going to bed but Waco decided he would go along to the smoker in the hope he would meet some fellow spirits to pass the night. He walked along the swaying aisles and across the platforms between the train's carriages. The city was gone from sight now and they were lulling out into open country again. He breathed in the air and grinned. If that was a big city he hoped such would never come to the West, and that he never need go to another.

Entering the smoker he found it still almost empty and his attention was drawn to the poker game. He moved forward and halted by the empty seat, looking down. Lou was dealing and Waco grinned as he noted the way the man held the cards, three fingers gripping the long edge, fourth around the front and holding square the short edge. Next Waco's eye went to the young man who sat alone. The two drummers were fleecing him, that was for sure. It was the sort of game a prudent young man would steer clear of; nothing but trouble and loss faced one sitting in on such a game.

'Room for players, gents?'

Lou looked up from dealing, taking in every detail of Waco's dress and his apparent youth. He read Waco as a cowhand returning from the big city, a young one and easy meat. His eyes, unused to looking for such things, did not see the bulge made by the gun. Waving a hand he cheerily said, 'Sure, friend. Set and play a few.'

Waco took the seat next to Keith Wellington with no idea who the young man was. Lou introduced himself, Keith and Joe just by their christian names and Waco told them the only name he'd ever known. He did not remember Molly's ex-fiancé's name or connect this young dude with him. He noted Keith was flushed and worried looking and could guess why.

Keith felt relieved when Waco sat in. The game was getting out of his depth and he was losing heavily. It was the opposite of the early stages when the stakes were low and his luck very good. Hand after hand came to him and brought in pot after pot. Then Lou asked if they could raise the stakes. From a friendly and harmless five to tenty-five cent limit it was now fifty cents to five dollars and Keith's luck had changed for the worse. Now he could rarely do anything right and was losing heavily. His suspicions were aroused but he could not get over the fact that he chose the cards.

Waco accepted the cards after Lou's deal and gave them an awkward overhand stack, the way the veriest amateur would handle cards. He offered the cards to Lou to cut, then dealt in a clumsy way which brought grins to Lou and Joe's face. He'd laid his money on the table and they were eager to add it to Keith's pile. It shouldn't be hard; a man who dealt in such a manner would not cause them any trouble.

In that casual stack Waco checked the cards and could see no sign of their being marked. That meant the two men were using other methods to take Keith's roll from him. He knew his awkward handling of the cards was lulling the suspicions of the two men. They did not guess he knew how to handle cards and knew more than a little of the ways of crooked gamblers. His eyes were alert. Without appearing to, he saw everything. He saw Joe make what appeared to be a nervous gesture, gently and quickly pull the second of his five cards out. Just an apparently casual pull but it told Lou, and Waco, Joe held a pair.

117

The betting went the rounds and Waco discarded his hand right off while watching him and in a casual move he extracted three jacks, laying them on the top of the deck. The move was done fast and unseen by any of the others. He waited for betting to end then asked, 'Cards gents?' hoping Keith held a pair and took three cards.

'Take three,' Keith answered.

Picking up the three cards Keith almost dropped them again. He was in the game with a pair of queens, now he held a full house, jacks and queens. Keeping his face impassive he managed to hold down his excitement as Joe took three cards and Lou two.

Joe grinned savagely. 'I've got them this time, boys. So run for the hills.'

'I never was any good at climbing,' Keith replied and opened the betting eagerly.

Joe's grin of triumph died an uneasy death as his three kings went under to the full house. He knew the chances of filling a full house from a three card draw were high. His eyes flickered to Waco but on the youngster's face was nothing but mild interest. Joe decided it was pure bad luck which cost him this sizeable pot.

The game went on. Keith took the next pot and Lou reached for the cards and dealt. There was nothing wrong with the deal that Waco could see but he noticed that Keith showed the signs of having a good hand. Waco wondered where this young man learned to play poker. He wouldn't last in a real rough game like this even without cheating. Waco once more discarded and Joe made a joking reference to it. At the same moment Lou fanned his cards out, tapped the top edge once in an apparently nervous move, then moved the third card up and down twice. Waco read the signal that Lou held three aces and caught Joe's almost imperceptible agreement that he held the fourth. Waco knew what was coming now; it was called the spread and an old gambling trick.

The betting in the game was brisk for Keith held a flush dealt pat and felt he had a better than fair chance of winning. He shoved up the betting cheerily and the other two went along with it. Joe folded his cards and grunted.

'This's too rich for my blood.'

Waco watched the cards falling in a pile and knew that only four were there, the fifth, the desired ace was palmed by Joe ready for use. Lou was holding his cards bunched together but he fanned them out as a man would when the betting was steep. When he folded them together once more he'd got one card palmed. His left hand dropped out of sight behind the table in a casual move and slid the card between his knees, holding it. Now he only held four cards and needed the extra ace his partner was holding out.

Lou took one card on the draw, laying his four in a neat pile before him. He grinned knowingly as Keith declined to draw and pushed his draw card on to the others. Keith pushed the betting some more then called. This was what Waco was waiting for, the moment of the spread. Lou turned his cards, still in one pile and said, 'Four aces.'

In a casual appearing move Joe reached across the table as if to spread the cards out, the palmed ace ready to drop into place. Waco moved fast, one hand shoving Lou's cards to one side, the other reaching for Joe's wrist. Fingers like steel clamps closed on the man's wrist and turned it, exposing the ace laying in his palm. Then Waco's other hand shoved the cards, showing four, not five laying there.

Joe jerked his hand free, dipping it into his pocket. The light of the smoker glinted on the shining steel of his razor as it licked out at Waco's face. The young Texan pitched sideways from his seat, the razor lashing over his head and ripping open the seat. Even as he fell Waco's right hand went across his body and brought out his Colt. The crash of the shot sounded louder than a cannon in the confines of the smoker. Joe rocked backwards, hit under the armpit by the heavy bullet and thrown back on to the seat again.

There was a thud and Lou crashed from his seat, a small light calibre Smith & Wesson revolver caught half out of his pocket. Waco came to his feet and grinned his thanks to Keith, whose help, via a well placed left fist, saved him from what could have been a ticklish position.

'Hold it!' Waco gave a warning as he lined his Colt on Lou who was clawing for his gun again. 'Let loose or I'll drop you and I've got me a permit to do it.'

Lou licked his lips. He still thought this was an easy mark cowhand here, one who'd made a lucky guess. He'd never seen a real fast man with a gun and did not have any idea how fast and deadly one could be. He still kept his hand on his gun, snarling, 'I'll get——!'

'Pouch it or I'll let you join your friend,' Waco answered, blue eyes never leaving the man ignoring Joe who was laying back with an arm which would never be of use to him again. 'You must think we were real easy, friend, trying to pull the spread on us.'

It was in that moment Lou realised that he was up against something more than just a dressed up cowhand. Here was a man who was a master with a gun. Then it hit Lou. A man who knew enough about the cheating trick called the spread, knew more than a little about cards. He knew far more than a man who gave a clumsy, overhand stack should know.

The few occupants of the smoker were on their feet now and the conductor forced his way through them. He came up, a big, burly man well capable ot taking care of himself. 'All right, all right. What's it all about then?'

Waco did not take his eyes from Lou, who still held his revolver, as he answered. 'These two tinhorns tried to take Chicago and me in a brace game. I caught them trying to use the spread on us. That gent there took his razor but I allow it's some too late for shaving. If the other don't let go of his gun I'll help him to. Me'n ole Colonel Sam.'

'Well, if it ain't Joe and Lou.' The conductor knew these two men from way back. 'Haven't I told you two not to use the train I'm conducting?' He put his hand under his coat and took out a revolver. 'Come on, both of you. Get down to the caboose. You're getting off at the next whistlestop.'

For a moment Waco thought Lou was going to argue the matter but the man was no gunfighter and knew the conductor was capable of either shooting him down or felling him with the barrel of the gun. He rose and helped Joe up. Then his eyes turned to Waco, full of hate. 'You should be throwing him off the train as well. He's a damn cardshark.'

'Me?' Waco grinned, it made him look about sixteen. 'I'm just a lil ole Texas boy who got lucky.'

'Yeah,' the conductor's voice was heavily sarcastic. 'You sure look it.'

The conductor herded Lou and Joe from the smoker with a warning that he would be back. Waco shoved the Colt back under his coat again and waved to the money on the table. 'There enough there to cover all you lost, Chicago?'

Keith counted the money and nodded. 'Enough and more. Do you mean they were cheating all the time?'

'Why sure. They weren't real good at it though.' Waco picked up the remaining money and made it into two equal piles. He took five dollars from each pile and scooped his share into his pocket, leaving the ten dollars and Keith's pile on the table.

The conductor returned and found the two young men seated at the table. 'You playing cards again?' he asked.

'Not me,' Waco answered. 'I only sat in to lend Chicago here a hand when the wolves were fleecing him. It was a real rough school you got tied in with, Chicago.'

Keith's face reddened slightly. His Streeterville Sporting Club training did not appear to be so good after all when a chance passing stranger could spot he was being fleeced. He kept his mouth shut for this young man saved his bankroll for him and prevented him from making a complete fool of himself. He could imagine what Molly would say if she'd met him and he confessed a couple of cheap crooks took all his money in an easily spotted card game.

The conductor grinned, eyeing Waco warily. 'Good, I wouldn't want a boy as smart as you taking up where Joe and Lou left off. They're good but you must be better, you caught them out.'

Waco took up the ten dollars, handing them to the conductor. He waved a hand to the roof of the smoker car where his bullet, after passing through Joe's shoulder was now buried. 'This'll pay for the hole I put in the roof.'

The conductor accepted the money, folded it and put it in his pocket, then turned and walked away. Keith turned to the tall, young man who'd come so suddenly into his life and did not know how to express his thanks. 'I don't know how to thank you,' he began.

'Don't try. I sat in for the laughs and made some money out of it. You headed west?'

'Yes, to the Ranse River country in Texas. I want to be a cowhand.'

Waco was naturally suspicious, more so when things were in the state that they were in Ranse River country. He wondered why, out of all the many miles of Texas this young dude was headed for the Ranse River country. He did not ask the obvious question for that would be against the etiquette of the land.

'You thinking of settling down there?' That much was permitted.

'Maybe. I'd like to be a cowhand. I can ride a horse and shoot.'

'There's just a bit more to being a cowhand than riding and shooting. You got any place in mind down there to work?'

'No.' Keith could hardly explain his true reasons for going to Ranse River, not even to this youngster who'd saved his bankroll. 'I decided to try and learn the cowhand business, maybe settle down out there and buy a ranch. I saw the Ranse River on the map and liked the sound of it. That's why I'm going there.'

Waco did not speak for a moment but his mind was working. He was suspicious of the other's motives. Of course the young man might be going innocently to Texas but there might be a more sinister motive. Waco was nearly sure he could lay a hand on the man who was behind the killing of his adopted father and the trouble in Ranse River Country. He could be wrong, this young dude might be the one. He made his decision right away and said:

'I work in the Ranse River country myself. Just been to Chicago with my boss. Come along and happen Rusty'll give you a riding chore.'

Keith thought this was a remarkable coincidence, meeting a man who was from the Ranse River Country. The offer of work was attractive. It might make Molly change her mind about him if she met him in Whittle while he was actually working for another ranch in the area. He did not connect the name Rusty with Molly. She'd talked about Mary Anne Catlan but Keith did not remember it. Nor did he guess Waco's real reason for offering him work was to keep an eye on him and have him where his movements could be watched. He gave his agreement to going along and seeing Waco's boss, expecting to meet a lethery cowhand.

The two young men made their way to the sleepers and Waco knocked on a door. A most unmasculine voice called out to know who was knocking.

'Waco and a friend.'

The door opened and Mary Anne looked out, her Merwin & Hulbert gun in her hand. 'Hey, lil brother,' she greeted. 'We were just set to go to bed. Who's your friend?'

'A tophand from Chicago, headed west and looking for a riding chore. I told him we'd likely be able to take on another hand.'

Mary Anne smiled, suspecting a typical cowhand joke. Waco looked serious about it, but he would even if it was a joke. Of course the other young man might be headed west and looking for work but the Ranse River country was not the best place for a dude to come in and start learning to earn his pay. The young man was well dressed and did not look as if he was coming west because he could not find work in the East. She decided Waco must have some reason for bringing the young man here. Of course, this might be one of his friends wearing dude clothes.

'All right, I reckon we could take you on, Chicago. I'm Mary Anne Catlan, the boss of the S.S.C.' She heard Molly getting up and coming towards the door. 'This is my friend and neighbour, Molly Wilmont.'

'I believe we've met.' Keith managed to retain control of his senses as he found himself facing his ex-fiancée. 'I think she dropped this the last time we met.'

Molly looked down at the engagement ring he held out and snorted angrily. 'What're you doing here?'

'Going west,' Keith replied.

Mary Anne smiled. She did not know if Waco guessed who the young man was. There was nothing to be gained in standing here talking. 'Come in, both of you.'

Keith entered the room, followed by Waco. Molly made no attempt to take the ring. Her eyes flickered at Keith's face and she asked, 'Just what's the game?'

'No game. I'm coming west to find work. Miss Catlan just hired me to work on her ranch.'

'She did, did she?' Molly growled. 'Well you're not working for any fat mantrap.'

'Fat is it, you scraggy hen!' Mary Anne yelled. 'Why for two cents I'd——'

'You'd what?' Molly was so mixed up emotionally that she did not know what to do or say.

'Come on, Chicago,' Waco said, grinning at the girls who were glaring at each other. 'This ain't going to be no safe place for a couple of innocent boys like us.'

Keith followed Waco from the room, was pulled rather, for he wanted to stop and talk with Molly. He did not realise until he was standing in front of the sleeper compartment Waco had reserved that he'd left the ring on Molly's bunk.

The two girls were now examining it and Molly smiled, her face showing her delight. 'He's coming with me, Rusty, he's coming with me.'

For all of that Molly was cool towards Keith the next morning and remained so until they reached the railhead in Texas. In the thriving, booming trailend town Molly decided that Keith must look like a cowhand, even if he would never make one. So Keith and Waco went along to a general store.

'You want a Stetson for a start, Chicago,' Waco stated and they made their way to the counter where such were on display. 'Buy the best you can afford, you'll never regret it.'

Keith bought the expensive and genuine Stetson Waco chose for him and allowed the young Texan to shape it for him. He put it on and tried to get it at the right jack-deuce angle over his eye. Then he chose a tartan shirt, Levis trousers and high-heeled boots. Waco was adamant on one point, the boots must be replaced by made-to-measures as soon as they got settled in Whittle. No cowhand worth his salt would wear ready-made boots. Spurs, the real, genuine Kelly spurs of Texas came next, bought from the store which could sell a man all he would need in clothing and gear. A saddle, bridle, reins, horse-blanket, tarp and warbag came next but one purchase Keith wished to make did not come off. Waco watched him buy a brand new, ivory-handled Colt Cavalry Peacemaker but drew the line at a ready-to-wear gunbelt.

'I'd like a gunbelt,' Keith remarked as they sat at the camp-fire on the first night of their trip to Whittle, after leaving the railroad and travelling with the girls in the rig they hired and the two men riding the horses which brought Waco and Mary Anne to the railhead. 'One like yours.'

Mary Anne laughed. 'That's a Gayline belt, Chicago.'

'Couldn't I buy one?'

'Not from Joe Gayline. He'll sell you a saddle, or a pair of his boots, if you'd got enough money to buy them. But he won't sell his gunbelts to anyone. He chooses the men whom he makes them for. I bet there aren't more than thirty of them in the West.'

Keith could read the pride in Mary Anne's voice as she told of the gunbelt her little brother wore. She was proud that he owned, wore and was a member of that élite group who carried the Gayline gunbelts. 'I could buy another,' he finally said.

'Sure, but get one made in Whittle. You might go all your life and never need a gun,' Waco told him. 'But if you need one, lord, you need it fast. A ready-made's the best way I know of getting you killed. Can you use a Colt?'

Keith rose, smiling. He was the best shot in the Streeterville Sporting Club and held the club record for pistol shooting. True, he'd been using a target-sighted Smith & Wesson .32 revolver then but he did not expect any trouble in shooting the .45 Colt. He asked for Waco to suggest a target.

'How about that tree?' Waco inquired, grinning, a grin

which was mirrored by the two girls.

Keith looked at the tree and smiled, Waco was picking a big enough target. It was probably the best he could do at a range of about twenty feet. Keith opened the loading gate and slid six fat cartridges into the chambers. Then he stood with his left hand on his hip, sideways to the target, feet placed correctly, right pointing to the target, left at right angles. He started to lift his right hand.

From his side came four rapid crashes, so fast that they sounded almost as one. Flame lanced from the gun which Waco held waist high, locked tight against his side while his right hand fanned the hammer. Keith gulped. He saw splinters kicking from the tree and then gazed down at the gun Waco held.

'See, Chicago,' Waco said, friendship in his voice, not mocking in any way. 'With a gun you've got to be fast.'

'Fast!' Keith gulped. 'I've never seen anything so fast in all my life.'

'Yeah, the boy's fast,' Mary Anne chuckled. 'There aren't many faster, are there, Molly?'

'I've never see faster.'

'There's three,' Waco said seriously.

'Who are they?' Keith wanted to know all he could about the West.

'Dusty Fog, Mark Counter and Doc Leroy,' Waco replied. 'Come on, settle down by the fire and clean your gun.'

They came into Whittle City in the early morning and rode slowly along the main street. Keith looked the part of a Texas cowhand, even sat his horse like one. He brought his horse to a halt and pushed back his hat. A man was coming along the street towards him. Keith stopped talking to the others and studied the man. Then he rode forward and halted the horse, looking down at Brarsand.

'Why, it's Mr. Jackson. I thought you were in Denver.'

Brarsand stopped in his tracks, his face, long schooled in frontier poker games, showing nothing of his thoughts. Then he looked up at Keith with the right expression for a man mistaken for some other person. 'Sorry, friend. You've got the wrong man. The name's Brarsand, I've never been to Chicago in my life.'

Keith frowned. He'd worked in his father's business and developed an ability to remember faces and names. It annoyed him that he'd made a mistake and of course it must be a mistake. Jackson was a gentleman, the Streeterville Sporting Club was exclusive and kept a high standard of its guests. This man here wore what Keith had seen to be the dress of a frontier gambler. He inclined his head politely. 'I'm sorry, sir. The resemblance is remarkable but I must have made a mistake.'

Waco was pleased that Keith said this. It saved him cutting in helping out. His eyes were cold as he watched Brarsand and the man looked back at him, then at the two girls.

'Haven't seen you around yet, Waco,' Brarsand remarked. 'I thought you'd be in to take that drink with me.'

'Would have, but I've been away. Took Mary Anne here over to the big city.' Waco gave the information to see how Brarsand took it. He was forced to concede the man held his emotions in perfect control. 'We went to fetch Molly here back home. Figgered she might be needed to look after things.'

Brarsand nodded in agreement. 'It's always as well to have the owner living on the property. Well, I've got work to do. Ladies.'

Raising his hat politely Brarsand walked on without looking back and entered the tavern. Waco watched the man go, noting that Brarsand stood at the door to watch them. Keith was still frowning. He shook his head at last.

'I could have sworn he was the man I met at the Sporting Club.'

'Who'd you think he was, Chicago?' Mary Anne inquired.

'A man called Jackson. I was introduced to him but Jackson came from Denver,' Keith replied as they started to move forward. 'Where are we going now?'

'To the livery barn. Molly and I want to borrow a couple of horses from Uncle Seamus and arrange for him to send this buggy back to the railead. Then we'll head for the S.S.C.'

Brarsand entered the saloon and looked around. There were

only three hard-faced gunhung men and his regular workers here. Jerking his head to one of the men, Brarsand gave orders as he came over. 'Get down to the livery barn, Ed. You'll find two men and two girls there. You'll know who I mean, one of them's that Tejano who shot Dave Tull. I want the other killed. Get both if you can but get the one wearing the tartan shirt first.'

The gunman turned and walked away and Brarsand called another over. 'Hank, head for the ranch. If Cholla is back bring his bunch into town. If he isn't bring every other man who's there.'

Della Christine joined Brarsand now, watching the men leave, curious. 'Where's Ed going?' she asked.

'There's a man in town who met me in Chicago,' Brarsand answered, then his face darkened. 'I made a bad slip. Said I'd never been in Chicago and neither of the men even mentioned they'd been to, or come from, Chicago.'

'They'll never notice it.'

'I've told you before, that Texas boy is smart, real smart. He knows I've made a slip. He's no fool and can think things out. I asked around town about him since he first came. Thought at first he was just a hired gun brought in to help the girl. He's more than that, he's Catlan's adopted son.' His face clouded for a moment. 'That letter, it means O'Dea or Waco was suspicious. Do you think they knew it was a forgery, Della?'

'I told you Doc Pilsener's the best of them all.'

'Yet they knew. I saw O'Dea and hinted I'd like to buy a ranch around here but he never mentioned the Lazy W. Thought the letter was delayed, or maybe lost. So I told him to let me know if he heard of one going around here. They must have been suspicious and Waco took the Catlan girl to Chicago to bring Molly Wilmont home.'

Della gulped. She was worried now. 'Do you think they found out who wrote the letter?'

'How could they. And if they did Pilsener's dead. Besides how could they find out about him. In the West Waco could, likely. But not in a big city like Chicago. I couldn't have found him without your help. No, they didn't know about Pilsener.'

Before Della could reply they heard shots and stopped talking, looking at the door and awaiting the report from their man when he returned.

Waco and Keith were standing by the corrals and watching the horses while the two girls made arrangements for mounts and the return of the buggy. To Keith's eyes the horses here were good and he said so.

'Sure, they're all right for what they're used for. They aren't cowhorses though. Say, who did you say you thought Brarsand was?'

'Jackson. I met him at the Sporting Club.'

'Who was he with?'

'Theo Benedict. The head of the Chicago–Texas Railroad. But it can't be the same man.'

'Jackson?' Waco rubbed his jaw. There was something worrying him, something he should know but could not just remember.

'Yes, but he came from Denver.'

Then Waco's tenacious memory got it. The register at the Reed-Astoria and a man called Jackson, from Denver who'd checked out the day the forger, Doc Pilsener died. He got something more, something Brarsand said there in the street. Mr. Brarsand was going to be needing to answer questions real soon. For all that Waco was cautious for he knew he could not handle all Brarsand's men alone. The best plan was head for the ranch, ole Red Blaze would—

Waco thrust out his hand, sending Keith staggering violently behind the water-trough. At the same moment Waco flung himself backwards, landing on his back, gun in his right hand as he rolled over. From behind them a gun roared and the bullet hissed between them. Waco was right out in the open and a clear target for the man who was flattened behind the wall of the livery barn. Waco expected to feel lead slamming into him and threw two fast shots which kicked splinters from the wall by the man's head.

Keith was shaken up by the push and his landing, but he saw where Waco was and knew his danger. Drawing his Colt he cocked it and came up, firing fast. Since Waco's showing him how to handle a gun Keith had made practice with his Colt. His bullet, fast taken, missed the man and he went down as lead slashed at him, sending water erupting from the trough as he lit down.

Lunging up Waco fanned off three fast shots, throwing the lead at the edge of the building. The gunman backed off, turned and ran for it. 'Keep down, Chicago!' Waco called, drawing his left-hand gun as he darted forward to the edge of the building, then leapt around ready to shoot. The alley between the livery barn and the next building was empty and the street was ahead. Waco went forward to look along the street but could see no one who might either be the gunman, or have seen him. The ground was too hard to allow him to read any sign from it.

Keith came up, gun out and ready. 'What was it?' he asked.

'Somebody tried to kill one of us,' Waco replied.

'You?'

Waco shook his head, turned on his heel and headed back to the corral. 'No, you!'

CHAPTER TWELVE

WACO MAKES FRIENDS

THE two girls, Seamus Reagan and Lafe Sanger came running up. Molly came straight to Keith and asked. 'What happened?'

It was Waco who replied. 'Somebody tried to kill Chicago. Get the hosses and let's get out of here. The sooner we're out of town the happier I'll be.'

'But what about the police when they come to investigate the shooting?' Keith, full of ideas about how things would be done in Chicago, asked, 'Shouldn't we wait to explain?'

'Nope. Lafe here's county deputy sheriff. He'll handle it for us!' Waco jerked his head to the corral. 'Pick two that can move, Rusty gal.'

'What was it, boy?' Sanger growled as the girls went to work, picking two horses and saddling them.

'Like I say, somebody tried to gun Chicago down.'

'Who?'

'You can call it as well as I can. If Talbot comes tell him we were having home target practice.'

Sanger grunted, looking Keith over. 'He's a greener, ain't he?'

'Sure.'

'Man'd say he makes him a tolerable amount of enemies, real fast. You sure it wasn't somebody after you?'

Waco's grin was mocking and sardonic as he replied, 'Could have been, 'cept I was laying right out there in the open and without cover, the man didn't try for me. He did for Chicago.'

The horses were saddled now and the girls mounted. Sanger scratched the side of his bristly jaw. 'Like to see you real soon, Waco. This wants some talking out.'

'Sure, I'd like to see you and Colonel O'Dea both. Where's

the Colonel at now?'

'Over to one of the nesters, holding a meeting.'

'We'll likely be back tonight, then I'll have something to tell you.' Waco swung afork his horse. 'See you later, Lafe.'

They were riding out of town before Keith spoke again. 'I think we ought to have stayed on and seen the sheriff or some other peace officer, Waco.'

'There's only Talbot, the marshal, and he's no use to us.' Waco answered. 'Besides I don't want you killing just yet.'

'That man must have been shooting at you, not me, I haven't been out here and don't know anybody——'

'You *thought* you knew somebody,' Waco pointed out.

Keith opened his mouth, then closed it again. The girls were now both looking hard at Waco and Molly snapped, 'Do you mean that man tried to kill Chicago?'

'Me?' Waco's eyes were flickering at the range around them, watchful and alert to locate anything which could spell hidden men. 'I don't think, not like you three smart folks. All I know is that if that hombre was after me he'd got a damned funny way of showing it. I was out in the open and a clear shot and it was still Chicago he went for.'

Keith frowned. He was not used to accepting being shot at. He thought the law should do something and said so vehemently. Mary Anne laughed and remarked, 'You listen to my lil brother, Chicago. He won't lead you more'n a couple of miles wrong. That damned Kansas sheep, Talbot, wouldn't do a damned thing.'

'But if he's a peace officer——'

'He's one of Earp's dirty crowd,' Waco growled.

'But Wyatt Earp is known as a great lawman,' Keith pointed out.

'Earp?' Waco spat the word out. 'He's nothing but a lying, bribe-taking, pious hypocrite. Him and all his bunch.'

Keith could see that Wyatt Earp was neither liked nor respected in Texas. Waco's view was typical of any cowhand who'd come into contact with the Kansas law and order crowd. He changed the subject again. 'Are you just going to forget it?'

'Nope, Lafe'll ask around and when we get back tonight he might know something for us.'

'What're you going back for?' Mary Anne asked grimly.

'To ask some questions.'

'Like which?' Molly wanted to know.

'For one like how Brarsand knew where Chicago came from without even asking. For another, what sort of gun Brarsand carries.'

'Then you think it was Brarsand who killed that man in Chicago?' Mary Anne said, her eyes on Waco's face. 'And killed pappy?'

'Yes, honey. That's what I think.' Waco reached over and gripped the girl by the shoulder. 'That's just what I think. Tonight Red, Doc, me and the boys are coming in to find out.'

'Not without the Lazy W boys,' Molly snapped. 'This's their fight, too.'

Before Waco could reply Keith said, 'Funny the way the smoke over there is acting.'

Looking up Waco saw the puffs of smoke rising into the air. It was not going up as normal smoke should but rising in separate, irregular clouds. Mary Anne noted where it was coming from and gasped. 'It's from the house.'

'Yeah, putting up smoke. It's an old trick we use at the O.D. Connected to call the hands in fast,' Waco answered, then set his Kelly petmakers to work sending his horse leaping forward. 'Let's go!'

The horses sprang forward in a racing gallop, each rider urging speed from their racing animal. Keith was a good rider, he'd always ridden, or all the time from when his father could afford it. He'd ridden in races but never before ridden with such urgency as now. He saw the set faces of his three companions and knew there was something badly wrong here. He was charging into another wild adventure, that he was sure of.

Doc Leroy was throwing a saddle on to his black and yelling to the other hands to saddle up when he heard the thunder of hooves and turned to see who was coming, for all the ranch crew were here now. He felt some relief when he recognised his friend, Waco. At a time like this Waco was worth three other men. 'Song,' he yelled. 'Throw a rope on Waco's paint.'

By the time Waco brought his sweating horse to a halt by the corral Song was holding the big paint stallion roped ready for him to slap a saddle on it. Waco made good time in saddling the big horse, then he slid the new rifle out and threw a bullet into the chamber. Keith was standing by the girls and Waco called, 'Take care of them, Chicago. Ride out.'

'Rustlers, took the stock herd. Red and Larry went after them,' Doc called back.

'Willie!' Molly yelled to a cowhand she knew. 'Give Chicago your hoss, I want you to go and fetch my crew here.'

Willie swung down from his horse. He did not like the idea of missing a fight but knew better than to disobey an order. Keith swung into the saddle of the horse and sent it after the rest of the party as they rode across the range. He thought how the West was just like in Ned Buntline books. He'd been shot at and now he was riding after rustlers with a posses of cowhands. This was the life and sure beat Chicago.

'Sorry about this, Willie,' Mary Anne told the cowhand. 'I'll get Lee to bake you a special apple pie and you'll get your chance tonight unless I'm wrong.'

Willie, a trencherman of note amongst the hearty eating cow-hands, was somewhat mollified by this promise of pie. He caught another horse from the remuda and was soon headed across country, making for Lazy W.

Waco brought his horse to a sliding stop and looked at the direction the tracks were leading. 'They're headed for the ford on the Ranse likely, Doc. We'd best make for it.'

'It's a big risk, boy. We might miss them, they might not have headed there.'

'We'll have to chance it. Let's go.' Waco swung his horse from the broader line of the herd and headed it in a direct line for the ford of the Ranse River.

Red Blaze left the Wilben house and raced for the foot of the slope, then up it, swerving as he ran. Above him the gunmen strained as they shoved against the weight of the wagon, trying to get it over the lip of the incline and rolling down to smash it into the front of the house. To their side Kell's eyes glowed murder as he sighted his Spencer rifle on the fast-running man. His rifle cracked loud, sounding even over the curses of the straining men and the crackle of flames as the hay at the front of the wagon blazed up.

It was close, very close. The shirt was ripped from Red's side as the bullet tore between his arm and side. Red did not halt. He kept on with his fast swerving run and heard the angry slap of another bullet passing close to him. Then he flung himself forward and landed behind a rock. Gripping both hands around the butt of his Colt, Red rested them on the rock and sighted up the slope. He'd seen Dusty Fog, Mark Counter and Waco do creditable shooting at ranges of up to a hundred yards by this method and made practice himself, but knew he was not good. He fired and saw the dirt kick up from the slope well below the wagon. The man with the Spencer sent another bullet down. Red swore after he felt the wind of it passing and knew he would get the next. For once in his life Red was cursing Christopher M. Spencer for devising such an efficient weapon. That .52 calibre rifle was not going to do him any good at all if it hit him.

He lined the gun again and from the corner of his eye saw the man standing, resting one foot on the rock and lining the rifle. Still Red would not allow himself to swerve from his attempt at stopping the men pushing the wagon. His Colt bellowed again and the bullet struck above the men. He saw them suddenly break away from the wagon and run for their horses, then heard the thunder of hooves. The man with the rifle suddenly spun around, his rifle fell from his hands and he toppled forward over the rock. Red came to his feet, recognising the men who came hurling over the top of the rim. His wild rebel war yell was echoed by Waco whose rifle saved his life.

One of the attackers went down before he even made his horse; a second crumpled over the saddle and slid down. The remainder headed off fast. Cholla Jocelyn did not worry about leaving bodies behind; he was only concerned with saving his life. His horse was running fast now and he knew he would soon be out of range of the Winchesters the cowhands always carried. He heard the slap of a bullet passing his head and urged his horse on at a better speed.

Waco swung down from his horse. It, like the rest of the cowhands' mounts was hard run and could not hope to catch up on the fast-riding men. One thing was for sure though. He knew that man who was headed out in the lead. There was one sure way to find out and seeing the wagon, guessing what it meant, Waco did not feel any scruples in shooting the man down. He brought up the rifle, lining it and firing fast, working the lever. That was where Jocelyn made the final mistake of his mis-spent life. He heard the bullet whistle by and thought one of the cowhands must be using either a Sharps or Remington singleshot. He was wrong. The rifle Waco was using had almost the range of the two old singleshots but with the magazine capacity neither possessed. Four times he fired, flipping open the lever each time to throw another bullet into the breech. On the fourth shot the man stiffened in his saddle and came off the horse to crash into the grass.

Doc Leroy gave a yell. The wagon was inching towards the edge of the slope now. Waco dropped his rifle and flung himself forward, bracing himself. He saw Keith and two of the cowhands leap to his side and even in that moment was pleased to see Keith was the first to move. The boy was going to make a hand, he'd make Molly a real good husband, the Lazy W a good boss.

The heat bit at the men as they strained to force the wagon back. Straggles of burning hay fell. But slowly, as more of the hands came up, the wagon was moved back to safety and Doc Leroy slid a rock under the wheel then watched the others step back. Waco wiped the sweat from his face and turned with a grin to grip Red Blaze's hand as the redhead reached them. It took a lot to put Red down for long and, despite his narrow escape, he was grinning broadly. 'Howdy boy, you came back just in time. Everything all right?'

'Sure, where's Larry.'

'I shoved him and the folks from the house down into the cellar. Reckon he'll be some riled when he gets out. But I couldn't let him come out here, one target was enough for them at one time.'

The cowhands crowded around Red; their jeering comments hiding their relief at finding both Red and Larry safe. They admired the redhead all the more for shoving Larry to safety before going out to almost certain death.

On the way down the slope Keith was introduced to the others, introduced in a far less formal manner than he'd been used to. He was given just the one name, Chicago, and no attempt was made to explain his presence. He did not know but none was needed; he was introduced by a friend and would be treated as an equal unless he gave cause for the cowhands to change their opinions. They'd noted the way he was the first to leap and help Waco hold the wagon and that was a point in his favour, that he'd ridden with them was another. He was accepted by the time they'd walked down the slope and reached the house. Then they heard hooves and fanned out fast, guns ready.

Colonel O'Dea, Smethers and several nesters came riding up. They all held rifles or shotguns and eyed the cowhands suspiciously. Waco lowered his rifle and stepped forward, 'Howdy Colonel.'

O'Dea looked first at the cowhands, most of them still holding their rifles ready, then glanced up at the burning wagon. 'What's all this, boy?' he asked.

'A bunch of guns attacked Wilbens.' It was Red who answered for the others. 'Waco and the crew came just in time to stop them rolling that wagon down there.'

'Now you're going in to ask Wilben for a drink?' a nester, a tall angry-looking young man, asked.

'We're surely hoping he'll get one for us,' Waco agreed knowing this man would be trouble unless handled correctly. 'Got to get him and his family out of the cellar first.'

There was danger in the air. The nesters were suspicious at finding the cowhands in such a position. The cowhands were angry. They'd ridden here, found two of their friends helping

137

to defend the house, and stopped the blazing hay-wagon. Now these nesters were coming here and looking for trouble. The cowhand was for the most part an amiable, friendly soul, but not when met with ingratitude such as this. There were angry mumbles on both sides.

Swinging down from his horse Colonel O'Dea walked forward and tried the Wilbens' door It opened and he looked back at the nesters. 'I take it as trusting, leaving the door open when they're fighting off an attack.'

The trapdoor lifted carefully and Larry, gun in hand, looked out. He grinned and called down, 'It's all right, folks. We can come up now.'

Wilben came out, rubbing his head. He walked across the room and gripped Red's hand in his own, shaking it. 'I'm riled with you, Red, so's Larry, what's the idea, shoving us down there while you go out and near get killed.'

'He wants to hog all the honours,' Larry scoffed, then as they reached the door they found the rest of the party standing around. 'You came back just in time, Waco.'

'Unless they were here all the time,' the nester who'd been doing all the talking growled.

Wilben stepped forward. He saw the anger on the faces of the cowhands and the suspicion of the nesters. 'Hello Charlie, how'd you lot get here?' he asked.

'The Colonel was seeing us over at my place. We heard the shooting and saw the smoke from that wagon of yours and came over in time to see the bunch making for the house.'

'The S.S.C. had a herd rustled, brought over here.' Wilben knew the young farmer, Charlie Hedge, did not like cowhands and knew why. He also wanted to end the suspicion between the cowhands and the nesters. 'The men who stole the herd stampeded it right at us. Red there, and Larry beat them here, turned the herd and helped me defend the house. If they hadn't been here I wouldn't have had a chance.'

'Why'd anybody steal a herd just to stampede it over your place?' Hedge asked, eyeing the Texans truculently.

'To cause trouble between the nesters and us,' Waco remarked. 'They knew some damned fool would want to make trouble if it happened. And they were right.'

'What's that mean?' Hedge snapped.

'Some damned fool's doing just that.'

'Charlie!' Wilben's snapped out word brought the others to a halt as Hedge realised what Waco meant. 'I know why you're against these men and I've told you I believe what they told us about Ben Silver. Red and Larry came here, risked getting killed to help us. Red stayed up on that slope until the right time to light the hay which turned the herd, Larry carried my Sandy down here when he was shot. Then when the men were going to send that burning wagon down here Red shoved all of us down into the cellar where we'd be safe. Then he went out alone and tried to stop them doing it.'

The other nesters listened to Wilben for they accepted his wisdom in anything. Waco watched them, then said, 'Talk's getting us no place. Let's get those bodies in here and take a look at their faces.'

The cowhands mounted their horses and headed to bring all the bodies in, laying them in a row along the side of the house. Waco went along, removing the masks. The first man was the one Red killed with the Kentucky rifle.

'That's one of the Kell boys,' Hedge growled. 'Bought that small spread from Brarsand. They've allus been friendly when I met them in town.'

'Was real friendly out there, too.' Red's tones were mocking. 'Where's the one who was trying to down me?'

They went along the line and then, as they reached the last, Waco pulled down the mask and nodded. 'Cholla Jocelyn. I thought it was him.'

'Brarsand's men. All of them, they were all hired by Brarsand.'

Waco looked at Hedge. 'Yeah, mister. Brarsand's men, all of them. We'd best talk this out.'

The men gathered round in a half circle. Waco stood facing them, one of the youngest here. Yet there was something about him which made the others listen to what he had to say. Before he started to speak he saw Sandy Wilben standing at the door of the cabin. The youngster's face was showing the same worry as it had that day in Whittle when Dave Tull died.

'First,' Waco said, 'I'm Sunshine Sam Catlan's boy. You know he was gunned down and I came to get the men who did it. I know why he was killed, or some of it. I know who ordered the killing.' Then he remembered something Keith said to him. 'Chicago, who was that *hombre* Jackson was with when you met him?'

'Benedict of the Chicago and Texas Railroad. They're thinking of running a spur line down to Whittle. He was after my father to invest in it.' Keith realised he was betraying a confidence, but knew that the betrayal was necessary.

'That's the reason. Look at the lay of the land. The railroad would come down here, through your land, across the Ranse and along the S.S.C., Lazy W line.'

Talk welled up among the nesters. This was news of vital importance to them, far more so than to the cowhands. Hedge spoke up, 'What do you make of it, then?'

'I've got it all now. Molly was in Chicago, my pappy killed. They thought either to scare Mary Anne out, or break her.' Waco went on to explain about the forged letter and what its consequences would have been. The men here knew the lay of the land and did not need it explained in detail. Then he told of his suspicions and the trip to Chicago to find proof. He finished off, 'That raid on the S.S.C. when the young nester was killed, that was to scare off Mary Anne or stir up trouble which would make her even more willing to sell. Who'd have known that pappy was going fishing that day?'.

'Nearly everybody who was in the tavern that night,' O'Dea replied. 'We'd been spinning windies about shooting and fishing and I bet Sam he couldn't take Old Mossyhorn. He said he'd be going out next morning. Brarsand was stakeholder for us. He said he'd go out and see how Sam went on.'

'Brarsand, did he go alone?'

'He said he never went. I went out and looked over the ground, there'd been four men there,' O'Dea replied.

'How'd one man take all three of them?' Waco shook his head. 'Pappy wasn't good with a gun, but him and the boys would be too much for one man.'

140

'Not if they were watching your pappy playing a big bass,' Red put in, pulling out his handkerchief and unrolling the phantom lure. 'I found a real big bass and took this out of his mouth.'

'And Sam's line was bust when we found him,' O'Dea said thoughtfully. 'Brarsand faded out of sight just after the shooting. Della told us he'd gone east on business.'

'Then Brarsand killed my pappy,' Waco took the phantom from Red. 'They'd all be watching the bass, not one of them would give him any attention. That was how he got them.' He faced Sandy Wilben, eyes hard and voice dropping grimly. 'All right, what happened the night Ben Silver was killed?'

Sandy gulped. His eyes went to his father but Wilben ordered him to tell anything he could. 'Ben and me went into the back room of the tavern. Dave Tull and the rest were there. They started to get us drunk, asked us if we wanted to go with them and have some fun. They were going to the S.S.C. to hooraw the hands. Ben was drunk, real drunk. I wasn't so bad and I got scared. Said I was going out back and just as I was going I saw Tull give Ben one of his guns. I lit out for home and left Ben with them.'

Hedge's eyes were hard. He turned to Waco and held out his hand. 'Looks like I owe you an apology, friend. It *was* just like you told it. What's Brarsand expect to gain by all this?'

'The railroad'll pay good prices for the right of way they want. That land of your'n be worth more'n it was solid gold. The man who owned it all and the two ranches would make him a fortune. That was what Brarsand would be aiming for. Same as the saloon he built. It wouldn't pay any in a small town like Whittle. But when Whittle boomed open with the railroad he'd be ready. He'd have the first and biggest saloon in town, he'd pile money up before the others could be built.'

'What're we going to do, friend?' Hedge asked for the other nesters. 'Ben Silver was kin even though I never saw eye to eye with his old man and I don't take to him being killed.'

'I'm going to town after Brarsand. There's one way to prove he killed the man in Chicago, look at his gun. I've never seen it, have any of you?'

There was a chorus of noes to this and O'Dea stepped up to stand by Waco. 'You haven't enough proof to take him into court, boy.'

'That's right. But I'll get it one way or the other.'

'We're with you,' Wilben spoke for the nesters.

'All right. We'll ride by the S.S.C., pick up more shells, then head into town. It'll be morning before we can do anything at all. Comes sun-up we'll go for a showdown.'

Mrs. Wilben came out. 'Coffee's on the boil, you'll have time for a drink before you leave.'

O'Dea came to Waco's side as the other men gathered together, talking. 'What're you going to do, boy?'

'What I came here for, get the man who shot down my pappy.'

CHAPTER THIRTEEN

MARY ANNE GETS HER CHANCE

BRARSAND got the news of the failure of the stampede from one of the men who'd escaped. He got it in the back room of his saloon early in the evening. 'Where's Cholla?' he asked.

'Dead and the Kell boys.'

'You get their bodies clear?'

'No boss. There wasn't time. The cowhands were on to us foot, hoss and artillery. We was lucky to get clear alive.'

'Were you?' Brarsand snarled. 'You damned, loco fool. I told you not to leave any bodies.' There was no time for re-crimination now, the young man called Waco would be coming here. Brarsand licked his lips. He thought fast. 'Get the place cleared of all but our men, then lock it up. I want all the boys ready for a fight. They'll be on us come sun-up at the latest.'

The occupants of the saloon were considerably surprised to be told it was closing down. Brarsand's men did not give them a chance to object but evicted them. Then the gunmen set to work to prepare the place for a fight that they knew must come. Della and the girls were set to work by Brarsand and within half an hour the place was silent, locked. Behind the walls the gunmen loaded their rifles and put out boxes of bullets ready for use.

At the Hood City saloon Lafe Sanger and Jabe Spencer were both surprised and pleased by the sudden influx of customers who'd been evicted from the tavern. Sanger was worried when he listened to a cowhand's voluble discussion on the fate which caused him to be turned out just when he'd hit him a lucky break. Picking up his hat the old-timer left the saloon and walked along the street towards the jail. He saw a man come out and recognised the angular shape of Talbot, the town marshal. Sanger was about to call out for, although he disliked the man, he always tried to co-operate with Talbot in any law matters. Then he shut his mouth for two more men left the jail, each loaded down with rifles, shotguns and ammunition. It was the supply held in the jail and Talbot should not be moving them at night. Sanger trailed the men around the back of the saloon. He saw a door open and Della Christine look out. The woman beckoned the other three men to enter and closed the door once more. Sanger went forward fast, his old Leech and Rigdon gun in his hand. He heard the click of the key turning in the lock and moved in closer to try and hear what was being said. All he could hear was a low muttering and drew back. Lafe Sanger was a wily old cuss and knew there was something afoot here, something concerned with Brarsand and that soft-talking young feller out at the S.S.C.

Della Christine locked the door and dropped the key into her bag along with the Remingtom Double Derringer which lay there. 'That all the weapons, Talbot?' she asked.

'Sure.' Talbot held down his anger at this woman talking to him in such a manner.

'Did anybody see you?'

'No.' Talbot would not admit that he clean forgot to see what was going on in town and did not know if he'd been followed. 'What's goin on?'

'We've got trouble,' Della was mocking. 'You're going to start earning some of your pay right now.'

Sanger withdrew, made his way home and collected his horse. He rode out for the S.S.C. and found a large party gathered there. All Mary Anne's crew, the nesters and the Lazy W hands were there, eating a hearty meal, checking their weapons and stuffing boxes of bullets into their pockets. It took Sanger only a few minutes listening to give his approval to the capture of Brarsand although he gave a grave warning about the state the saloon was in.

'They'll take some getting, boy,' he finished.

'I know, but we're going to get them.'

Mary Anne and Molly came over as the men mounted. Waco gripped the girl by the arms and kissed her. 'You stay on here, Rusty gal. We can handle this one without your help.'

Mary Anne nodded with surprising mildness. Waco was expecting violent objections from both girls at being left out of things but they were not raised. Molly kissed Keith, the engagement ring once more on her hand. 'Take care of yourself,' she said.

'I'll do just that.' Keith held her tight to him.

The men mounted and Waco gave his last orders. 'Remember, we'll get all round the place in the dark. Don't start in to shooting until it's light enough to see who you're shooting at. If any of them come out try and rope them. But don't take chances, you're up against trained gunhands. Shoot if you have to and shoot to kill.'

Mary Anne and Molly watched the men riding out and waited until the hooves faded into the distance. They stood side by side and finally Mary Anne spoke. 'Lil brother said we'd got to stay out here out of the way, didn't he?'

'Sure, and Chicago. We wouldn't want to do anything they didn't want us to, now would we?'

'We sure wouldn't.' There was a light in Mary Anne's eyes. 'A woman should always do what the menfolks tells her.'

'Sure.' Molly took a rope from the corral side. She went over to the corral and deftly built a loop, sending it snaking out over the head of a horse. 'Now isn't that strange, I caught a horse.'

Mary Anne was also building up a noose and caught her dun. They worked fast, throwing saddles on the horses. 'I bet Susan Mae's scared to death. We're her friends and should go and comfort her.'

'Why sure,' Molly agreed. 'One must stick to one's friends, mustn't one.'

With this kind thought in mind the girls rode for town, keeping well behind the men, and on reaching it sneaked around the back of the O'Dea place where a handful of pebbles thrown at the window woke Susan Mae O'Dea up. She came down, opened the door and allowed her friends to enter;

they went to her room without waking the rest of the house. Then Molly and Mary Anne told why they were here. Susan Mae offered to let them stay here in her room from where they should have a fair view of the fight.

Unsuspecting that the girls were in town, Waco put his men out around the saloon, moving them in under the cover of darkness and the waiting with the patience of an Indian for the morning. The sun came up, the shadows of the night faded back and in the cold grey light of the dawn Waco called, 'Brarsand! Brarsand. We got your men.'

'So?' Brarsand called back.

'Are you coming out or do we have to come in and get you?'

'Come and get me!' Brarsand was scanning the street. He could not locate any of the attackers.

Red Blaze, Spencer carbine in hand, darted forward to the side of a house and dropped behind the porch along with the two cowhands who were already there. Larry Beaumont grinned at Song. 'They sent us a loader, Song. Hope he don't get in the way.'

Song eased himself up to reply. The side window of the tavern broke and a rifle roared. Song slid down again, a hole through his shoulder. Red's carbine lifted and roared back, then from every side, every window of the tavern, came the thunder of shots. Larry pulled Song to one side and was about to say something when Song yelled, 'Up there!'

Turning, Larry saw a man with a rifle at one of the upper windows of the saloon. The young cowhand whirled fully around with his rifle raising and crashing as fast as he could work the lever. On the fifth shot he saw the man stagger backwards holding his face. 'Got him!' he whooped.

'Throw enough lead at them and some of it's bound to,' Red scoffed, levering another bullet into the chamber of his Spencer, then drawing the side hammer back. He sighted carefully on the lower window and promised he'd make anyone using it sorry. Then he remembered something. 'Watch the upstairs windows, Larry. How's Song?'

'Needs some help. Where's Doc?'

'Him and Waco are up there, between the Wells Fargo office and the store.' Red swung around as he heard someone coming. It was the Reagan brothers, each carrying a Springfield carbine. 'Howdy gents!' Red ducked as a bullet from the lower window narrowly missed his head. 'One of you help Song there?'

'Sure boy,' Seamus Reagan agreed.

'Good!' Red came up fast, his old Spencer roared just as the man at the window appeared for another try.

'Bet you missed,' Song muttered. The pain of his shoulder was intense but he held down any sign of it.

'I ain't you,' Red scoffed. 'His rifle's out there and——'

The rest of the words were cut off by the spat of a bullet near his head and the deep boom of Reagan's Springfield. A hole was in the wood of the porch about three inches in front of Red. He looked down at it then asked. 'What did that?'

'Mice,' Larry answered.

Waco and Doc were in a safe location, by the side of the Wells Fargo office. They knelt there with their rifles and watched Red further along. The saloon was surrounded now and from all sides came the flat crack of rifles and the deeper roar of Colts. The barking of the cowhand Winchester was backed by the deeper roar as Colonel O'Dea cut loose with his double-barrelled Colt rifle, and the heavy boom as Sanger brought his Sharps Old Reliable into the game. Word passed around the town in the night, alerted every citizen and they were all here, fighting along with the cowhands and the nesters against this man who'd tried to take over their town. From the saloon windows rifles, revolvers and shotguns answered the fire of the cowhands. Lead slashed the street and tore through the air, whining ricochets went off and occasionally men were hit.

'Reckon we can get them out, boy?' Doc asked.

'Sure, might take us some time. Depends how they are for food and water.' Waco lined his new rifle at a man who was showing too much of himself. The rifle crashed and the man spun around, out of sight. 'We can't rush them, that's for sure.'

147

'Yeah, that's for sure. Could try their own game on them if we can find a hay-wagon.'

'We're not that kind,' Waco answered. 'Besides, there is no way we could get one up there. Those guns won't stand by and fight if things go wrong. They'll want out of it.'

In the saloon Brarsand was thinking the same thing. His men were hired guns and they would not stand by him if things were going really bad. He turned to where Della and her girls were hidden behind the bar.

'Della, get those girls out of here. The Texans'll let them go through. You go with them, I've got something for you to do.'

'What?' Della was relieved to be getting out of the saloon for bullets were flying freely inside.

'You'll all go right across to the Wells Fargo office. Take some money with you and slip out the back. Go to the post office, you'll have to go round the back, by the livery barn, and send a message to the sheriff in Hood City. Tell him to come here.'

'What good will that do?' Della ducked as a bullet came through the window and smashed the bar mirror.

'It'll take him two hours at most to get here with a posse. I'll give myself up to him. There's nothing they can prove on me, nothing that a good lawyer can't break for me. I'll let him take me in.'

'Will that help?'

'Sure. That Texas boy, Waco, he'd kill me out of hand, but not if the sheriff's here. That way I'll get a trial, I wouldn't if they got in here.'

Della picked up her bag and opened it. She went behind the bar to take money from out of the cash drawer, then picked up the Remington Double Derringer and placed it on top. She turned and called the girls to her, then nodded to Brarsand.

Waco saw the handkerchief waving at the end of a rifle barrel and poked through the window. He yelled for the other men to stop shooting and as the noise died down went on: 'Giving up, Brarsand?'

'No, sending the girls out. I wouldn't want them killed by

148

your bullets.'

'Good enough, send ahead!' Waco gave his consent for he did not want any of the women hurt.

The batwing doors opened and the saloon girls came out, one after the other. Waco watched them, suspicious of Brarsand's feelings for the welfare of the girls. They crossed the road and entered the stage office, Della last, closing the door behind her.

'How about you, Brarsand?' Waco called. 'You giving up?'

From the window where the flag of truce came a rifle barked in reply and once more the gunfire shattered the silence of Whittle's streets.

Della Christine ignored the other girls as they clustered at the windows of the office, looking out. She crossed the room and went around the counter, opening the back door and stepping out. All the Wells Fargo people were in the fight and no one challenged her as she walked along behind the houses. She did not know if Brarsand's idea would work but she did know one thing. It was time she changed her affections again. When she'd sent off this message she meant to go back to the office and when the stage came in get on it.

She was walking between the livery barn and the corrals now and would cut between the houses, then to the post office. There she would either bribe or threaten the owner into sending the telegraph message to the sheriff. It was then she was aware that someone was running after her and swung around. Sudden hate welled up inside her. It was that damned Catlan girl.

Mary Anne Catlan and the other girls, Molly and the two O'Dea's were watching the fight from a safe place. The girls wanted to do something to help but none of them had any idea what. They might be able to fetch ammunition if any was needed but that was about all. It was then that Mary Anne saw Della leaving the Wells Fargo office by the back door. Turning without a word to her friends Mary Anne set after the blonde woman for she knew that Della was up to no good. Mary Anne ran along the back street and at the livery barn saw Della turn. There was no time to say anything now. The blonde was opening her bag and Mary Anne knew it was not to look for face powder.

Diving forward Mary Anne locked her arms round Della's waist and staggered her backwards. Della lost her hold of the Derringer and the bag. Her hands drove down, digging into Mary Anne's hair, pulling hard at it. Mary Anne gave a howl, let loose of Della's wrist and was pulled erect. Then Della let loose of the hair and swung a punch which smashed into the girl's cheek. It was a hard punch, harder than Mary Anne had ever felt. She crashed into the corral fence and saw Della, face contorted with hate, hurling at her.

They met like two enraged wildcats, tearing at hair, kicking, swing wild punches, oblivious of everything but their hate for each other. Della fought with the savage skill gained in many a bar-room brawl and Mary Anne fought back with the strength of a wild tomboy. They tripped and went rolling on the floor. Neither could gain the upper hand for long enough to make use of it. Della's dress, not meant to stand up to this kind of treatment, split at the seams and was torn off as they thrashed over and over but she gave it no thought. Mary Anne was luckier; she was still wearing her shirtwaist and jeans, and high-heeled riding boots on her feet.

Rolling apart, gasping for breath, they came to their feet. Mary Anne's shirtwaist was torn open, blood trickled from her nose and her left eye was swelling but she flung herself at Della without any hesitation. They tangled again in a wild, kicking mêlée and reeled back. Mary Anne yelled as she was pushed into the water-trough, her head forced under the water. Della leaned on the girl, holding her head down, feeling her struggles.

Mary Anne fought for breath. She brought her legs up around Della's waist and crossed her ankles, then tightened. The girl's legs were powerful, toughened by hours of riding, even in her eastern school. Della gasped as the crushing clamped on her. She fought to hold Mary Anne's head under the water but the power of those legs made her relax. Mary Anne forced herself up slightly then was pushed down, her hands trying desperately to tear away Della's grip. It was then she remembered that the water-trough had a plug in the bottom to allow it to drain. Letting loose of Della's hands, lungs bursting, Mary Anne felt for the plug and finally got it in her hand. She pulled hard, the plug came free and the water started to rush out. Mary Anne gasped in the air. Della screamed as the spur on Mary Anne's boot caught her. Her grip relaxed on the girl's throat and Mary Anne got both feet under Della's body, then shoved.

Staggering back Della tripped and sat down. Weakly, Mary Anne rolled herself from the water-trough and clung to it gasping for breath. For a moment they stayed like it, then Della rolled over and grabbed for her bag. Mary Anne did not hesitate. She flung herself forward, landing on the other woman and grabbing her wrist, holding the hand from the bag. Della fought back. Neither was screaming now; they were too short of breath for that. Coming up they staggered dazedly then Mary Anne caught Della a haymaker which rocked the blonde backwards. Della hit the corral rail and slid down to her knees, the bag just under her head. She looked down, then realised what it was. Weakly she reached inside, the Derringer came out and she started to lift it.

Mary Anne was almost exhausted but her pain-drugged mind was still working well enough to warn her of her danger. She staggered forward even as the sobbing Della started to raise her weapon. In a desperate move Mary Anne lashed up with her foot, the toe of the riding boot catching Della under the chin. Back snapped her head. She rocked over and hit the corral rail, the Derringer falling from her hand. She hung there for an instant then slid sideways. Mary Anne dropped forward and gripped Della's tangled, dirty blonde hair to smash her head into the corral rail. She did not know what she was doing. It meant nothing to Mary Anne that Della was unconscious.

'Rusty, stop it!' The voice seemed to be coming from a long way off. 'Rusty, stop it. You'll kill her.'

Hands were gripping Mary Anne. She tried to strain against them but she was too exhausted and allowed her three friends to pull her away from the limp, unconscious woman. She slumped down sobbing as the reaction set in. Molly snapped an order to the O'Dea girls to get a bucket of water.

It was some minutes before Mary Anne was able to take notice of what was happening. Then she sat on the water-trough and gasped in air while the other three worked on Della. The blonde was conscious and sat with her back to the corral. There was fear in her eyes. Mary Anne forced her aching body up and went forward.

'Don't let her touch me!' Della screamed. 'Keep her away from me.'

'All right,' Mary Anne looked down at the sobbing blonde. 'I want some answers and I want them now. What is it all about?'

The scared Della talked; told how Brarsand learned of the branch line of the railroad. She'd met him in a Kansas cattle-town and they'd come down here. It was Brarsand who'd killed Mary Anne's father, then found out too late about Mary Anne being in school. He'd been to Chicago to sound out the chances of Molly selling her place out. When he learned she would not he'd located Della's old boy friend, Doc Pilsener, who'd forged the letter telling Colonel O'Dea to sell. The idea was just as Waco figured it, to cut off the headwater of the Ranse River and break the nesters. When this failed he sent his men to stir up trouble between the S.S.C. and the nesters.

Mary Anne, aching in every fibre of her body, could still feel admiration for her little brother and the way he'd worked all this out himself. Then she looked down at Della. 'What were you doing back here?'

Della licked her bloody lips and gasped, 'Running out. I've done with Carl.'

'Running out, huh?' Mary Anne looked around and realised the direction Della had been headed. It was then she proved that not only her little brother could think things out. 'All right, girlie. What did you want at the post office?'

Della tried desperately to bluff. 'Post office?'

Mary Anne clenched her fists and snapped, 'Stand her up, girls.'

Molly and the O'Dea girls started to drag Della to her feet

but the blonde had taken enough punishment for one day. 'Don't hit me! I'll tell you. I was sending for the sheriff. Carl's willing to give himself up to the sheriff.'

'Why?' Mary Anne relaxed, bent and picked up the bag, opening it wide and removing the money, then the key which was underneath.

'His men want to quit. They'll hang on until the sheriff comes, but no longer.'

'Where's this key belong?'

'The back door of the saloon,' Della whimpered. 'Do not hurt me any more. Leave me alone!'

This last came in a scream as Mary Anne reached for Della. 'Get back down there.' Pulling the ripped shirtwaist into some semblance of order and modesty Mary Anne gave Della a shove. 'The boy'll want to know what you just told me.'

CHAPTER FOURTEEN

WACO PAYS HIS DEBT

'HEY, boy!'

Waco twisted around at the words, his eyes taking in Mary Anne's dirty, bruised and dishevelled appearance. 'What're you doing here?' he asked grimly. 'I thought I told you to stay at the ranch.'

'Yeah?' Mary Anne answered, bristling. 'Well, it's a good thing we didn't.' She jerked a thumb over her shoulder and indicated the even more bruised, battered and half-naked Della. 'She was going to send a telegraph message for the sheriff. I caught her.'

'Sure looks like you did, Rusty gal.' Waco grinned at the girl. 'I should have known better then try and stop you coming in. What's it all about?'

'Brarsand's the one we want. Della told us all about it.'

'Looks that way. What'd she say?' Waco asked.

'Brarsand's men want out. They're only sticking because they think the sheriff'll be coming to get them out.' Mary Anne glanced at the saloon. 'Reckon they'll not be sticking at all if they know Della didn't make it.'

Waco agreed with this. The men in the saloon, faced with a long drawn battle with the townspeople, would want to be out of it. Some of them just might stick but the majority would come out of Della's Tavern like weasel-chased rabbits. He did not know what the girl was thinking of doing and would have stopped her if he'd guessed. Before he could say or do anything Mary Anne pushed Della out into the street in front of her. 'Walk!' she snapped. 'Right in front of the saloon.'

Della staggered forward at Mary Anne's push, stumbling

154

blindly along. The firing died down for the men would not risk shooting a woman. Waco drew in his breath; he watched Mary Anne shoving Della along, making for the jail. Red Blaze also saw and darted across the street, around the back of the Wells Fargo office and came up to Waco. 'What the hell?' he asked.

'They'll be coming out any time now,' Waco answered. 'Get set.'

The two girls were just past the saloon when the batwing doors were flung open and a man erupted, gun out. He raced forward but went down under a hail of lead. Then more men came out, some came shooting and were cut down by the attackers, others threw aside their weapons and ran across the street to be taken in charge by the men who gathered.

Time dragged by slowly and the saloon was silent. Waco called, 'Brarsand, come out!'

If Brarsand expected to make Waco rush blindly in he failed badly for the youngster was no fool. Turning to one of the men who'd come out he asked, 'How many stayed on with him?'

'Talbot and one more, they're in the front.'

Waco handed Keith his rifle and checked over his Colts. Red and Doc were watching him and Molly took the key Mary Anne relieved Della of. 'This's the key to the back door. Rusty gave it to me.'

'Give me your hat, boy,' Red ordered. 'I'll move out so he can see it and keep them watching the front. You go around the back. We'll give you five minutes.'

Waco handed Red his stetson and Red laid his own on the sidewalk and pulled the black hat on. He stepped forward and Waco called, 'I'll give you five minutes, Brarsand, then I'm coming in after you.'

Saying this he turned and moved back, then bending low so that he could not be seen he darted across the street and between the two buildings. There were no windows on the bar side here and only one door which Waco guessed would be locked. He wondered where Brarsand's two remaining men were. One would be upstairs most likely, probably on this side

155

and covering the street. By hugging the wall Waco should be able to keep out of sight. He reached the end of the building and moved along keeping flat. The back room was empty except for a man who lay still on the floor. Waco saw that through the broken window as he went by to the door. He inserted the key, standing to one side and turning it slowly. The gun came into his right hand as the lock clicked and he gently eased the door open. There was no sound from the room, no shot, no alarm. Drawing his second gun Waco went in fast but in silence and halted just inside with guns ready.

The man on the floor was dead, shot by a heavy rifle. Waco turned and waved back the men who came from the houses behind the saloon and ran forward to help him. This was a personal matter now. Brarsand was the man who killed Sunshine Sam Catlan and tried to ruin the S.S.C. or scare Mary Anne from her home. Brarsand was Waco's meat, the man he'd ridden from the O.D. Connected to find.

Crossing the room on silent feet Waco holstered his left-hand gun once more and gripped the knob of the door leading into the bar-room. This was the time of danger. If the door was locked he would be forced to kick it open and alert them, but it would do no good to hesitate now. He twisted the knob and pushed the door slowly.

Brarsand was standing with his back to Waco, looking at the batwing doors and lining his revolver ready to shoot down the first man through. Waco was about to lunge forward when he saw the bar mirror's reflected view of the room. Apart from a man who lay by a broken window he could see no one. The stairs leading to the first floor and the balcony were deserted, yet at least one man should be there.

It was then Waco detected a movement, caught it reflected in the mirror. Talbot was crouching behind the bar, ten-gauge shotgun in his hands, ready to turn loose the murderous charge when the batwing doors burst open. Then Waco saw the black hat moving, accompanied by another, white hat. Red and Doc were moving in and he must take a hand.

'Brarsand!'

Waco yelled the word and flung himself forward. The big

man started to turn, his gun coming up. Waco's right-hand Colt crashed, throwing lead into the bar, shooting as fast as he could thumb the hammer. There was a roar from the shotgun as Talbot stiffened up into view then went down again.

Brarsand came round. He was fast but not fast enough. The revolver in his hand roared, flame licking at Waco as the young man flung himself to one side. Even as he went down Waco was shooting, his left-hand Colt thundering. Brarsand rocked on his heels, his gun crashed once more tearing a furrow in the floor by Waco, then the youngster rolled right over and fired as he landed on his stomach. A hole appeared between Brarsand's eyes, the big man going backwards, his gun flying from his hand. The thud of his body hitting the floor was echoed by the crash as Red and Doc burst through the batwing doors.

A man came into view, leaping from a side room to the balcony at the head of the stairs, his gun slanting down. Doc Leroy brought up his Colt fast, firing almost without aiming it seemed. The man was flung backwards by the impact of the shot. He crashed into the wall and slid down, the gun dropping from his hand.

Silence fell and the smoke of the burnt powder slowly dispersed. Waco got to his feet, walking to the man who'd killed his adopted father. He bent down and picked up the revolver, noting the awkward-looking butt and the cylinder which was slightly shorter than that of a Colt. He turned to hand the gun to Red. 'Take this for Ole Devil. He doesn't have a Webley R.I.C. in his collection.'

'He's the one, is he?' Red asked.

'Sure's he's the one. We'll let Ed Ballinger know we got the man who killed Doc Pilsener.'

'How about you, boy?' Doc inquired, for their business here was done now and the O.D. Connected might need them again.

'Reckon old Rusty gal can handle things here herself. Her and Larry between them,' Waco replied and grinned. 'Sure be good to see Dusty, Mark and Lon again.'

The three young men walked towards the door of the saloon

as men came crowding in. Waco stepped out and looked to where Larry Beaumont was talking to Mary Anne and hanging a blanket around her shoulders. The youngster smiled. Mary Anne would be all right. She wouldn't need him here now. He'd paid his debt to Sunshine Sam Catlan.

THE END

General

- [ ] 552 98789 1   INVESTING IN MAPS (illustrated) *Roger Baynton-Williams* 125p
- [ ] 552 08768 8   SEX MANNERS FOR OLDER TEENAGERS (illustrated)
  Robert Chartham 30p
- [ ] 552 07950 2   SEXUAL BEHAVIOUR   *Dr. Eustace Chesser* 25p
- [ ] 552 08805 6   WHO DO YOU THINK YOU ARE?   *Dr. Eustace Chesser* 25p
- [ ] 552 98572 4   NEE DE LA VAGUE (illustrated)   *Lucien Clergue* 105p
- [ ] 552 08745 9   MAGIC AND MYSTERY IN TIBET   *Alexandra David-Neel* 35p
- [ ] 552 08800 5   CHARIOTS OF THE GODS? (illustrated)
  Erich von Daniken 35p
- [ ] 552 08861 7   THE AUTOBIOGRAPHY OF A SUPER TRAMP
  W. H. Davies 40p
- [ ] 552 08677 0   ON THE EDGE OF THE ETHERIC   *Arthur Findlay* 30p
- [ ] 552 07400 4   MY LIFE AND LOVES   *Frank Harris* 65p
- [ ] 552 98748 4   MAKING LOVE (Photographs)   *Walter Hartford* 85p
- [ ] 552 08362 3   A DOCTOR SPEAKS ON SEXUAL EXPRESSION
  IN MARRIAGE (illustrated)   *Donald W. Hastings, M.D.* 50p
- [ ] 552 98247 4   THE HISTORY OF THE NUDE IN PHOTOGRAPHY
  (illustrated)   *Peter Lacey and Anthony La Rotonda* 125p
- [ ] 552 98345 4   THE ARTIST AND THE NUDE (illustrated)   105p
- [ ] 552 98862 6   INVESTING IN GEORGIAN GLASS (illustrated)
  Ward Lloyd 125p
- [ ] 552 08069 1   THE OTHER VICTORIANS   *Steven Marcus* 50p
- [ ] 553 08664 9   THE HUMAN ZOO   *Desmond Morris* 35p
- [ ] 552 08162 0   THE NAKED APE   *Desmond Morris* 30p
- [ ] 552 08765 3   THE HERMIT   *T. Lobsang Rampa* 30p
- [ ] 552 08880 3   THE THIRTEENTH CANDLE   *T. Lobsang Rampa* 35p
- [ ] 552 08630 4   BRUCE TEGNER'S COMPLETE BOOK OF
  KARATE (illustrated)   *Bruce Tegner* 40p
- [ ] 552 98479 5   MADEMOISELLE 1 + 1 (illustrated)
  Marcel Veronese and Jean-Claude Peretz 105p
- [ ] 552 08807 2   BIRTH CONTROL NOW AND TOMORROW
  Clive Wood 30p

Western

- [ ] 552 08532 4   BLOOD BROTHER   *Elliott Arnold* 40p
- [ ] 552 08783 1   HELL IN THE PALO DURO No. 66   *J. T. Edson* 25p
- [ ] 552 08841 2   BAD HOMBRE   *J. T. Edson* 25p
- [ ] 552 08673 8   NORTH TO THE RAILS   *Louis L'Amour* 25p
- [ ] 552 08840 4   UNDER THE SWEETWATER RIM   *Louis L'Amour* 25p
- [ ] 552 08857 9   REVENGE No. 11   *Louis Masterson* 20p
- [ ] 552 08858 7   STORM OVER SONORA No. 12   *Louis Masterson* 20p
- [ ] 552 08876 5   OUT WEST Vol. 1   ed. *Jack Schaefer* 25p
- [ ] 552 08877 3   OUT WEST Vol. 2   ed. *Jack Schaefer* 25p
- [ ] 552 08812 9   SUDDEN MAKES WAR   *Oliver Strange* 25p

Crime

- [ ] 552 08826 9   MURDER WITH MUSHROOMS   *John Creasey* 25p
- [ ] 552 08875 7   THE TWISTED WIRE   *Richard Falkirk* 25p
- [ ] 552 08809 9   MADRIGAL   *John Gardner* 25p
- [ ] 552 08739 4   TRAITOR'S EXIT   *John Gardner* 25p
- [ ] 552 08780 7   DEAD MARCH IN THREE KEYS   *Norah Lofts* 25p
- [ ] 552 08640 1   RED FILE FOR CALLAN   *James Mitchell* 25p
- [ ] 552 08839 0   TOUCHFEATHER TOO   *Jimmy Sangster* 25p
- [ ] 552 08758 0   SURVIVAL . . . ZERO!   *Mickey Spillane* 25p

*All these books are available at your bookshop or newsagent: or can be ordered direct
from the publisher. Just tick the titles you want and fill in the form below.*

CORGI BOOKS, Cash Sales Department, P.O. Box 11, Falmouth, Cornwall.
Please send cheque or postal order. No currency. and allow 5p per book to cover the
cost of postage and packing in the U.K., and overseas.

NAME ....

ADDRESS ....

(JAN. 72) ....

A SELECTION OF FINE READING
AVAILABLE IN CORGI BOOKS